Lesbian Love Songs

Lee Cushing

Published by Lee Cushing, 2023.

LESBIAN LOVE SONGS

First edition. April 19, 2023.

ISBN: 979-8215667668

Written by Lee Cushing.

Music Of The Heart

Mitchell, twenty years and full of life, living her best life as a popular Rock star, with her boyfriend, Andrew. They've both been together since high school and they never for once broke up. But, Mitchell noticed the way her body reacts to beautiful ladies around her. Countless times, she would playfully fondle with ladies boobs and ass.

Andrew, on the other hand, had been suspicious of her behaves and relations with ladies. He confronted her about her sexuality and if she was really into him. Mitchell, was with him, not because of love or anything, but because she was afraid of walking up to a lady and telling her she loved him. The fear of rejection made her stick with Andrew, till she would get her own lover.

On one of her tours, as a rock star, she met a gorgeous Australian Chick, with rosy lips and flushed cheeks. She was taken by her beauty, and made a promise to herself to ask her out. Unknown to her, Andrew had seen the lady earlier and asked for her contact. Before her show ended, Andrew was already getting down on the Australian Chick, while Mitchell performed.

Mitchell caught her boyfriend having hot and mind blowing sex with the new girl she was thinking of having for herself. She composed herself and silently went back to her fans to sing again.

In her mind, she had plans of breaking Andrew's heart by asking Dora, the Australian lady out. Luckily for her, Dora came all the way from New York city to Los Angeles to watch Mitchell perform.

After two months of secretly dating her, Andrew invited Dora to his house, on the pretence of introducing her as an artist. Mitchell acted innocent and welcomed Dora, and sang with her. With an opportunity to snatch her from his boyfriend, she chose to work with her, due to her amazing voice.

Two weeks later, mitchell invited Dora over for Dinner in her house, despite knowing of the affair between her and her boyfriend.

With Andrew out of town, she made her intentions known to Dora. She spoke with a convincing attitude and body language that left Dora in both shock and amazement. As she spoke, her concentration was on her beautiful eyes and rosy lips.

Dora could not resist Mitchell's beautiful blue eyes. Her eyes were the kind that caught your attention, easily without any difficulty, immediately drawing you in with their depth and intensity. Her eyes were bright blue, sparkling like daylight in a clear summer sky, casting an undeniable radiance across her face and her entire body.

Her eyes were almond shaped, with a slight upward tilt at the outer corners that gave them a subtle, exotic quality. Her long lashes, black and with mascara well applied, battled severally, matching her black eye shades, casting an entire different colour and life to her already radiant face, when she blinked.

As she spoke to Dora, Dora was lost in the world of her amazing eyes, staring back at her, like two yummy berries. Her eyes conveyed a sense of warmth and life with openness, as if she were inviting you to her innermost thoughts and ideas. Her gaze, focused and direct, bore right through Dora and captured her heart.

As she spoke, she refused to break eye contact, so as to achieve her aim. Her soft eyes which looked gentle and innocent, spoke of mischief and a hint of playfulness. The way her lips curled up, showed she has secrets she was willing to share with Dora.

Her eyes was a stunning combination of beauty, power, love, warmth and mystery, making Dora feel simultaneously drawn to her and captivated. With Dora's eyes off Mitchell's, she slowly dragged her gaze down to her inviting lips.

Her lips were full and luscious, with a natural pout that looks like it was asking for a long sweet kiss. Her lips slowly merged the gloss on her lips, in a seducing manner as she spoke. They looked real soft and drew her gaze. Her lips were perfectly lined, to make them feel and look smaller.

A rosy lush pink, delicate like the petals of a flower and special like a Lilly. They had a smooth, silky texture that looked irresistibly touchable.

She smiled as she spoke, with her lips curving into a perfect arch, showing their natural balance and beauty. As she opened her mouth to speak, her lips moved with a fluid grace, shaping each word with clarity and smartness.

To her lips, was a subtle, natural shine, with exception of the gloss, making her lips more shinny, which made them more tempting, begging to be kissed.

The way her lips expressed emotions made them stood out, in special way. When she smiled, laughed or giggled, they would stretch into a wide, toothy grin that lit up her entire face. They would purse into a mischievous smirk, when she was playful, hinting at a wild side lurking beneath her elegant exterior.

Overall, her lips were a sensual, expressive feature that perfectly complemented the rest of her beauty.

Dora patiently listened to her, and when she was done, she took a bold step towards Mitchell and with a big smile on her face, landed her lips on hers, taking her by surprise.

Mitchell froze. She was expecting her to react in another way, but this. Even after telling her she knew of the affair between her and her boyfriend, all she could do was give her own response with a brain melting kiss, long enough to make a lady drool.

Some minutes after, they broke the kiss and Dora finally spoke up.

" I've fallen on love with you, since I started listening to your song. I had to somehow make myself noticeable the night you came to perform in Los Angeles. Andrew was just a silly excuse to get to you". She said and drew Mitchell in, again for another round of kiss.

Andrew was shocked to see that Mitchell packed out of their apartment before his arrival from his journey. He could not deduce her reasons for such an action, but he was glad at the change in event.

Thinking he would be able to finally being Dora into his apartment as his official girlfriend, he sent a message to her, informing her of Mitchell's move.

Mitchell, on the other hand, sent a text to him, too, telling him of her decision to dump him, as she has found someone else, who was ready to make her happy for the rest of her life. He got the message without any sad feeling, but was rather happy.

He was expected Dora to come over that afternoon, but was amazed to see his ex girlfriend and Dora, alighting from the car. They both wore matching mini black leather pants with black winter boots and a strapless top, with most of their busty boobs, outside, as they elegantly walked into his apartment while holding hands.

They even had their hair styled same way, in a brown colour and a touch of wine by the side, with the waves of their hair, bouncing as they walked. Their nails were properly manicured and their faces slightly powered with blush on their cheeks.

They both looked so happy together, as they walked hand in hand, to meet Andrew.

" You thought you could dump me? Ha, I beat you at your own game" said Mitchell.

" Yes, my baby did. We both used you, now you have nothing to gain. We are on love with each other and will always remain in love" added Dora.

Andrew was left speechless, as he watched the two lovers kiss each other passionately in front of him. It was too much to bear, to loose two gorgeous women. He remembered how he once worshipped Mitchell's perfect curves, until he met Dora, who was a super model. Dora's curves were more perfect, due to the fact that she worked out daily to remain fit, for her modelling work. He never thought his girlfriend was into ladies. He could not utter any word, as he continued to watch the two, still kissing in his living room, not minding his presence.

He had always thought Mitchell would be his main girlfriend, while he pursues after other ladies, without her consent. Rather, he was the one that got played by Mitchell herself.

" You mean, you girls are lesbians? You don't need any man in your life?" asked Andrew, finally, interrupting the lovers kiss.

" What does it look like to you that we are? Sisters? We are in love, of course, thanks to you, for bringing us together" replied Dora.

" I think we should get out of here, before he spoils our mood, babe" Mitchell said. They both agreed and left Andrew in his confused state. They decided to go to one of the most expensive restaurant and have some lunch. They also used that opportunity to know more about each other.

Dora, came from a middle class family, in Australia. Her parents could not afford to send her to college, so, she opted for a modelling work. Her captivating figure and radiant skin, made her quickly popular in the industry.

Her narrow waist and wider hips gave her body a perfect shape of an hourglass figure, which can create a sense of femininity and allure. Her flat tummy, housed a little belly button which made her hips and waist more approachable and inviting. She has a slender and tall body, with a narrow waist and wider hips that are proportionate to her overall body shape.

Her skin was smooth and flawless, as if it had been delicately polished to a fine sheen. Its fair, porcelain-like complexion was soft and supple to the touch, with no blemishes or imperfections to be seen. In the light, it glowed with a gentle radiance that seemed to emanate from within, lending her an otherworldly beauty that was both striking and captivating.

Her steps, were gracefully managed, as she walked upright and nice, like the model she is, with her backside, bouncing to the rhythm of her steps as she moves.

Her nice and healthy skin made her stand out among other models and in a matter of months, everyone in the industry wanted her to model for them. Her smiles, dissolves the hardest heart, and made the weariest mind merry. She laughs with the grace of royalty, spreading cheers everywhere.

Her long hair stopped directly on her back side, with butterfly clips adorning her hair. She has a cat like eyes, which only shone brighter in the night like the cat. Her elongated and slightly upward eyes, sparks like pearls when it is lined with her favourite liners.

The irises of her grey eyes were always large and bright, with a vibrant colour that stands out against her milky skin tone. Her dilated pupils, adding to the seductive and mysterious quality of her eyes, changes colour at times, adding captivating beauty, drawing the viewer in with a gaze that is intense.

Mitchell, was chanced to go to a college, but soon started pursuing music as a career, once she graduated. She was pretty equipped with a singing voice.

Her tiny voice, made people love her, more than other rock stars. She became popular after her first hit song, talking about love and heartbreak.

Dora and Mitchell were both happy to find each other, as they both filled the empty holes in their heart. Together, they would do lots of shopping, mainly on what they need, in preparation for their special red night.

Their special red night was a day, finally chosen to do things they have been imagining to do to their bodies. They bought the longest and biggest dildos, some cuffs and blindfold, just to make everything memorable.

Together, they made their home a place of love, place of hope to look forward to.

Mitchell and Dora set up their house on a lovely weekend, like they were expecting someone important. They both made dinner, in their panties, with a thin piece of clothing covering their boobs, as they worked. Occasionally, they'll stop for a quick kiss and ass grabbing, with smiles.

Dora and Mitchell both were already madly in love with each other, as they continued to love together as couples. Their passion for each other only grew stronger, everyday, even without having intimate knowledge of one another.

After few weeks of living together, they made decided to spend some quality time together. Since they were of different races, they made dishes of their nationality and choice. Mitchell made a dish of Roast beef and Yorkshire pudding. Since it was a special occasion, she made the special dish which only required slow cooked beef, served with crispy and fluffy Yorkshire puddings.

The beef was seasoned with a mix of herbs, salt, and pepper and roasted to perfection. She made the pudding batter from eggs, flour, milk, salt, and baked in the oven until golden brown. She proceeded to serve it with roasted potatoes, vegetables and a rich beef gravy.

While Dora made a sumptuous meal of meat pie and tomato sauce. Apart from being a model, she once worked as a cook, baking pies and cakes. She was pretty good in the art. She made the pie with a flaky pastry crust and is filled with savoury minced beef or lamb, onions, and a blend of spices. The filling was typically slow- cooked to allow the flavours to develop and was then spooned into the pastry case.

The pie was baked until the pastry became golden brown and crispy. She served it with tomato sauce, which is a sweet and tangy condiment made from tomatoes, sugar, vinegar, and spices.

Soft music played in the background, as they cooked. The air was filled with the scent of lavender and vanilla, and the room was decorated with fresh flowers and flickering candles. A plush couch covered in soft blankets and pillows, inviting you to sink into its comfort, was placed at the centre of the living room for their comfort.

They both had a quick shower before settling down to devour their food. They were half way into their meal when Mitchell's manger suddenly came to her apartment. He was directed by Andrew to Dora's house, since he could not find her at his apartment.

His unexpected interruption made things a bit awkward, as the two lovers had not made their love affair public. Mitchell's manger, Mr. Ralph, came to discuss about her next show, but was hooked down by the sweet smelling aroma of food, coming from the dinning table. To have a taste of the food, he intentionally prolonged his discussion with her, at the dining. The lovers, made eye contact, while Mr. Ralph spoke, non stop.

They could not wait for him to leave them alone, as Dora placed her hands on the bare and fleshy laps of Mitchell. She traced her hands up and loosed the buttons of her bum short, dumping her hands into her panties. Mr. Ralph was too occupied with the food he was eating, which made his ears blocked to the faint gasps and moans of Mitchell and the uncomfortable silence in the room.

" Excuse me, Mr. Ralph. I need to make a call with my client" Dora said as she excused herself from the room, to go and make a fake call. She winked at Mitchell, who just smiled without knowing what was coming.

Dora walked majestically into the room with her ass almost peeking out from her shorts, only to reappear again. This time, she was barefooted and slowly crawled into the dinning room, without Mitchell and Mr. Ralph knowing, since they were both lost in the world of business. Dora quietly went under the covers of the table, towards Mitchell.

She was pretty good in it, as she was unnoticed by the duo. She placed her hands on Mitchell's laps and squeezed lightly. Mitchell could not help but yelp at the unexpected touch from under the table.

" What is the matter, Mitch?" enquired Mr. Ralph as he looked up to see her frightened face. She looked under the table and saw Dora, with her finger on her lips, telling her to keep shut.

"I just panicked unnecessarily. I was tickled by the other end of the table cover" she lied as she raised the end of the table cover up. Mr. Ralph believed her and continued his discussion.

Under the table, Dora, kissed her Laps, at interval, as she made her way up to her already loosed short. She made an attempt to drag it down, and was helped by Mitchell as she raised her butt up a little to aid in removing her shorts.

Dora moved closer to have a deep smell of her freshly shaved juicy pot. She inhaled and breathe out on her pussy. She massaged her pussy slightly with her hands, rubbing and teasing. Before she could do anything, Mitchell was already producing some liquid, which made her extremely wet and ready.

Dora made her sit we, with her butt at the edge of the chair, while she spreads her labia with her hands, giving her a proper view of her pink entrance. Dora smiled coyly as she made contact with her tongue on Mitchell's throbbing clit. She could hear her let out a moan, and swallowing a sigh, as she licked on her exposed clit.

She particularly concentrated on her clit, to make her feel an extreme pleasure. Mitchel could hardly comprehend with what Mr. Ralph was saying as she was lost in pleasure. Her fists were clenched and her eyes shut, tight while her insides coiled up from the intensity of the pleasure.

Dora opened her mouth wide to take on the juice dropping from her centre. Mitchell reached her hand down and grabbed Dora's hair tight, pulling her in, for more as she was about to reach her climax. Her grips on her hair was pretty tight, as she could not moan out. Her veins popped out well, from her denial. She placed one hand over her mouth, to avoid the suspecting eyes of Mr. Ralph, who was not yet ready to leave.

After ten minutes, Mitchell found a way to send Mr. Ralph away from the apartment. She was successful after a lot of attempt, and once he was gone, she dragged out Dora from under the table, as she landed her lips on hers, kissing her ferociously without breaking the kiss. She ripped off the remaining piece of clothing on both of them, while still kissing, as they made their way to the bedroom.

Mitchell laid on the bed, to allow Dora continue her violence on her, as she arched her back in pleasure at the contact of her pretty tongue in her tight hole. Her hands unknowingly grabbed the sheets from the bed, pulling them to herself as her tongue did their work on her swollen, sensitive clit. " Oh, pl, please. Don't, don't , s...s..stop" she managed to say as Dora continued to lick her. The pleasure was too much for her to handle, as Dora rolled her tongue in her hole. Her gaze met Dora's , making her blush and throwing her head backwards, as Dora spread her legs for more access.

Dora licked her soft Sore core, as she raised the upper part of her body, gripped the bed sheets tight, and opened her mouth without producing a word, as she reached her climax. Her breathing was heavy and fast, as her heart raced uncontrollably. Dora crawled up to her and whispered into her ears, " tonight, I'll finally claim you as mine. Your body is meant for me tonight, and I will do things unimaginable to you, till you scream out your lungs". Dora proceeded to kiss her ear lobes, licking as Mitchell moaned out. She moved a little down to the exposed part of her long neck, sucking and licking on a particular spot, which made Mitchell go crazy.

Dora's hand slowly moved all over her body, stopping at her erected nipples, and pinching them real hard. Mitchell was in shock as she moaned out and squirm under Dora. She positioned herself on top of Mitchell, grinding her hips on hers, as she held on to her inviting boobs. She placed her mouth over one of her boobs, sucking on her already active nipple, making Mitchell more responsive as she increased her pace in raising her hips to meet Dora's.

As she sucked, her hand reached down to find her soft core, again. She rubbed her hands lovingly and in a torturous manner, making Mitchell gasp for breathe, as she was out of breathe from the impact and pleasure she was receiving from both her hand, down in her panties and her mouth, sucking and biting her boobs, hungrily.

She got down and licked and sucked, while nibbling her throbbing clit again, as she felt breathless making her scream out. Mitchell was lost in pleasure, as Dora stopped pleasing her with her tongue and sharply inserted two of her fingers into her hole. Mitchell flinched from the mixture of pain and pleasure she got from Dora's fingers as she moved in and out of her p*ssy slowly.

" Oh, yes, yes. Keep going. Yes, that's way, uhm, don't s..stop. Faster, faster" moaned out Mitchell with her eyes tightly closed and her hands grabbing the sheets of the bed. Dora increased her pace, as Mitchell's hips grinded quickly against her fingers, coming in and out of her. She was enjoying the pleasure she was getting, as she kept moving her hips against her fingers.

" Don't stop, yet....go, faster, faster. I'm cumming now, I am cum..cumming" she screamed out as her legs shook uncontrollably. She released lots of milky juice from her cunt, as she also squirt all over the bed. She remained on the bed, as her body still was in shock from her journey to cloud nine.

To relax for, they both went into the living room and sat down on the couch, with Dora carrying a tray of wine and cheese. She poured each a glass of wine, and they share the delicious cheese while chatting and laughing together.

They watched a movie together, as they sat cuddles on the couch, enjoying the warmth emanating from their bodies, and the intimate atmospheric created. The soft lighting, soothing scents and gentle music all combined, to create a romantic and lovely space where they both connected more, enjoying each other's company.

Mitchell found her way into Dora's red lace panties, and inserted one finger into her wet p*ssy. The kisses they shared while watching a romantic and highly erotic movie made them both wet and horny. Mitchell could no longer resist Dora's figure, as she pinned her down to the love couch, with her fingers going in and out of her wetness, extracting a moan or two from her.

Mitchell positioned herself well, and lifted Dora's two legs, placed them on her shoulders, as she licked her wetness clean, without stopping. She flipped her tongue over her p*,ssy long and hard like a dog would do, licking and sucking her deep.

Her breathe was hot against Dora's little p*ssy, making her entire body shiver in pleasure. Mitchell looked up to see Dora's face, shut and lost in pleasure with her hands, holding firmly to her breast, squeezing as Mitchell licked her out.

Mitchell dipped her fingers again into her opening, and added a touch of her tongue, as her fingers moved in and out of her, while her moans echoes all over the apartment.

Mitchell coiled up her fingers, in Dora, getting her tender spot, and giving it a proper tug with her fingers, making her squirt all over the couch while cumming.

The lovers slept, interlocked in each other on the bed, after a night of pleasure. Dora was the first to wake up, and she made her way into the kitchen to prepare a sumptuous meal, of Mitchell's favourite dish.

The aroma of the scrambled egg woke Mitchell up to the morning sunlight filtering through the window, Her nose got stuffed with the delicious aroma of breakfast wafting into her bedroom. She was about to leave the bed, when she saw Dora coming towards her with a tray, their eyes bright and their smile warm.

The tray was filled with an array of mouth-watering treats. There was a cup of steaming coffee and a glass of freshly squeezed orange juice, and a small vase of fresh flowers adding a touch of colour to the already beautiful tray.

On the tray, there was a plate of perfectly cooked scrambled eggs, lightly seasoned with salt and pepper, and garnished with some chopped chives. Next to the eggs, there was slices of crispy bacon, and golden brown toast, with a side of butter and jam.

Dora, with a big smile plastered on her face, sets the tray down on the bed. Mitchell felt the warmth and comfort of the soft sheets beneath her. She took a sip of the coffee, feeling the warmth spread through her body. After, she took a bite of the scrambled eggs, savouring the creamy and savoury flavour, with her eyes beaming like daylight. The bacon was crispy, well made and salty, perfectly complementing the eggs.

Mitchell enjoyed her breakfast, with Dora sitting beside her, chatting and laughing, making her feel loved and appreciated. The morning sun streams through the window, casting a gentle glow across the bedroom, creating a warm and cozy atmosphere.

Mitchell took her time with the breakfast, enjoying the moment and feeling happy for the special person in her life. The breakfast in bed, marked the beginning of a long romantic affair between the lovers, as they ended up, fondling each other's breasts and kissing, passionately.

They both made their way into the bathroom, to have a shower together. "I want to treat you well and right. I want to make you feel loved and special, because you are the one my heart chose" Dora whispered into Mitchell's ears as the shower dropped down upon them both, as they were locked in a tight embrace.

" Let me do everything I have ever imagined, let me do them to you" added Dora, as she took the soap and rubbed it on Mitchell's back in a seducing manner. She took the foamy substance and applied it to her breasts, pressing them hard, making Mitchell feel a mixture of pain and pleasure from her hands.

As the water splashed down on them both, running down into the sink, Dora traced her way down to Mitchell's opening, dipping her fingers in her, making her gasp, as her fingers created a sort of friction between them.

Mitchell had to place her hands on the wall, for support as her legs could no longer support her weight, as she was getting drilled from beneath.

" Hold on, I need to get something" said Dora as she kissed Mitchell's lips, before exiting the shower. She went into her wardrobe, and brought out a big vibrator.

She steeped I to shower, and knelt in front of Mitchell, while she slowly eased the vibrator into her, and activating the machine.

Mitchell could not control herself as she screamed out, in pleasure as the vibrator drilled her home, making her insides tingling. It Vibrated aggressively in her p*ssy, making her legs shake uncontrollably, with her eyes rolling back into their sockets.

She continued to scream endlessly as the vibrator expanded her hole, coming in and out of her pussy. For five minutes, Dora kept it in her pussy, while she fingers her ass hole.

Noticing she would likely cum, soon, Dora stopped the vibrator and replaced it with her warm mouth, sucking and licking her clit, and within one minute, Mitchell unconsciously squirt into her mouth with cum, running down Dora's face.

Dora was not offended or moved, as she licked her clean, with Mitchell still vibrating and trying to catch her breathe, while the shower ran down her body. Once they were outside the shower, they both wore a nice short and a light top and sat outside, taking in the beauty of the day.

They just used part of the morning to get more closer It was a morning that felt like a dream come true, a morning that they never wanted to end.

As they sat there, holding hands and watching the sunlight, Dora turned to Mitchell and said, "I know this might sound cheesy, but I feel like I'm living in a fairy tale with you."

Mitchell smiled and leaned in to kiss Dora. "Me too," she said. "But it's not a fairy tale, it's real life, and I wouldn't want it any other way."

They sat together in silence for a few moments, taking in the beauty of the moment, as the sky formed different shapes.

Finally, Dora broke the silence. "I just want you to know how much you mean to me," she said, turning to look at Mitchell. "You make me feel like the luckiest person in the world, and I don't ever want to lose you."

Mitchell smiled and pulled Dora into a tight embrace. "You'll never lose me," she whispered. "I'll always be here for you."

Mitchell made up her mind, that it was finally time to make the world know of her choice in sexuality.

As they watched the sun coming up, fully and stretching it's long fingers of warmth over the while land, Dora and Mitchell cuddled, feeling the warmth and comfort of each other's love. It was a perfect moment, a perfect start to a bright, perfect day, and they knew that they had found something truly special in each other.

Chase

The luxurious fashion magazine bustles with shoppers in the heart of the city, but a young lady stands out from the crowd. She has just stepped out of the building, her stylish dress and expensive handbag oozing class and announcing her status to the world. As she makes her way down the lonely driveway, the click of her heels echoes off the pavement.

Despite the glamorous surroundings, an inexplicable sense of foreboding gnaws at her mind. She quickens her pace, resisting the urge to look over her shoulder because that would only spook whatever she suspects is following her. As she approaches the driveway, she looks back but sees nothing but the shadowed walls of the buildings surrounding her. She shakes off the eerie feeling and continues walking.

The sky has hues of red and purple as the sun sets over the city. Her surroundings grow darker with each step, amplifying the unsettling atmosphere. Suddenly, a rustling sound from behind catches her attention. She spins around, heart pounding in her chest, but sees only the fashion magazine's grand entrance and the display window showcasing the latest trends.

Feeling uneasy, she increases her pace, the heels of her designer shoes clacking loudly on the pavement. The feeling that she is being followed pokes her being as the hairs on the back of her neck stand on end. She hears footsteps closing in and turns around sharply, but sees only the deserted street stretching out behind her.

She breaks into a jog, her heart pounding in her chest. The surroundings blur past her as she runs, but the footsteps persist, growing louder with each passing moment. She turns the corner, but her heel catches on the curb, and she tumbles to the ground. As she looks up, she sees a shadowy figure towering above her, letting her catch a view of a glinting object in the dim light.

The young lady's heart races as she stares up at the shadowy figure. She tries to scream for help, but her voice is lodged in her throat, and all she can manage is a feeble whimper. The figure steps closer, and she can feel its breath on her face. Her mind races, and she tries to recall any self-defense techniques she might have learned. But her thoughts are jumbled, and her limbs feel heavy as if frozen.

The figure looms over her, and the glinting object in its hand grows more prominent. She tries to crawl backward, but her body refuses to obey. The figure moves closer still, its features obscured by the dim light, and the young lady can feel her life flashing before her eyes. She wonders if this is the end, if her family will ever find out what happened to her, if her killer will be caught, or if justice will ever be served.

Her eyes grow glossy with tears boiling in them, pleading wordlessly. She wants more for herself, ending like this is not what she envisioned for her life.

Suddenly, her mind turns to why anyone will want her dead, a thousand and one questions racing through her mind as she tries to compile a mental list of people, she might have wronged in a way two. Everything she can think of is way too trivia to cost her life. A few broke-shaming banters, a few heartbreaks, a number of painful withdrawals, a little childish bullying. Nothing serious occurs to her but her life is about to be snuffed out of her for reasons she cannot comprehend.

Finally, she lets out a deep breath, not wanting to hold anything back in what she knows is her last seconds on Earth. Her tears reach out the surface, staining her well made-up face as they travel down.

Chase Munroe, a young and ambitious lesbian is overjoyed to receive the news of her promotion to police detective. She is fully aware of how deserving she is of the promotion on account of how it is the culmination of years of hard work, dedication, and an unrelenting pursuit of justice. Chase has always known that she is destined to make a difference in the world, and this is the opportunity she has been living for.

Beaming from ear to ear, she feels a sense of immense gratitude wash over her being as the thought of how much work she has put in and how it has yielded the results she expected fills her mind. If gratitude had a face, it would be identical to hers as a consequence of the recognition she has received. She can't help but compare herself to the other officers she started off with, who have yet to land any higher positions, and this makes her even more grateful for the success she has achieved.

As she walks through the precinct's hallways, she allows herself bask in a sense of pride seeing how high emotions have become. She looks around at her colleagues, who are all busily engaged in their work, and can't help but feel a sense of belonging.

It takes all the strength in her gut to refrain from screaming out of excitement. In this moment, she feels like she is finally in the right place, doing exactly what she is meant to do. It's a rare feeling that she has never experienced before, and she relishes every moment of it.

As she looks around, she notices how hard everyone seems to be working, all focused and determined to achieve their goals. She considers the atmosphere is challenging, but she feels energized by it. She knows that this is where she is supposed to be, and is grateful for the opportunity.

In her heart, she knows that there will never be a better alignment of anything in the universe than this moment. It's a present-day happening that she'll always cherish, knowing that she's doing exactly what she's meant to do

An overwhelming sense of excitement and gratitude for being in the right place, doing the right thing, churns within Chase. She knows that it is a rare feeling and a present-day happening that she'll never forget.

The hustle as a fresh out of oven detective is bound to begin after now, leaving her with only today to relish and savor the feeling that comes with a promotion. She knows how necessary it is for her to observe her colleagues intently so as to learn the style of the house, as well as avoid any form of drama that will bring her out in the wrong light.

Chase does not let the joy make her forget that the promotion comes with its own set of challenges. As a young, openly lesbian detective, she knows that she will have to work twice as hard to prove herself in a male-dominated profession. But she is determined to succeed, no matter the obstacles in her path. She knows that her sexual orientation does not define her, and that her dedication and skill will earn her the respect she deserves. With a deep breath, Chase steps into her new office, ready to take on the challenges of her new role, and perhaps, on the world from this new, little corner of hers.

As she settles into her new role as a detective, eager to prove herself and make a meaningful impact on her community, she does not care if it will require her spending long hours in the office, poring over case files and analyzing evidence, or her hitting the streets, working tirelessly to solve crimes and bring perpetrators to justice. She has been ready from the first day she signed up to join the force, she has been ready to put in the work even before her new promotion. The promotion has only presented itself as an opportunity and a platform for her work to receive the deserving recognition.

A sense of responsibility works within her, creating the need to make her colleagues and superior take notice of her dedication and skill, for her to earn the respect of those around her.

Early the next morning, she arrives the office, prepared to receive her first assignment, without letting the smile on her face fade. Chase had been careful to not show up a little earlier than the other colleagues who has been there before her as a first impression. She shows up early, but not in the fashion of newbies who are overly eager to get noticed.

She says a few hellos on her way to the office, bearing in mind how important it is that she cultivate a friendly relationship with her coworkers.

"You're Chase, right?" one of the guys asks with a smile.

"Yes," she says, returning the smile.

"I am Michael," he stretches his hand for a shake.

"Nice to meet you, Michael," she beams, as she shakes his hand.

"My pleasure," he responds with a little chuckle. "Welcome."

With that, they both continue their journey in the opposite directions.

"Detective, I have a new case for you," her superior says as he hands her a file containing her first assignment after sending for her immediately, he arrived.

She accepts it without questions, and skims through it with all carefulness, ensuring she grasps the main details in it before looking up to receive further instructions

"It's a mysterious murder of a young woman near a fashion magazine. We have very little information at this point, but we need to find out who did this and bring them to justice," he says with a note of apology in his tone. "We are counting on you to figure it out, we have faith in your abilities, Detective."

She takes a deep breath and nods before heading back to her office with the file.

In her office, she begins by reading through the file intently, trying to write a few points down all to no avail. She notices how sparse the details are, and this begins to cause a rising sense of frustration in her. She has very little information to go on which will require her to work thrice as hard uncover the closed book, as well as demystify the murder.

"I don't understand," she says to no one in particular. "How can I solve this with so little to go on?"

Her frustration is palpable but she knows that she has to start somewhere. She begins to read through the file again, looking for any clue that might help her solve the case. And after several hours of intense focus, she finally finds something that catches her attention. It is a detail that she had missed before, a small piece of information that could potentially be a crucial clue in the case.

With renewed energy, she continues to pour over the file, taking detailed notes and mapping out a plan of action. She is aware that if she is going to get anywhere with the case, she will need to follow up on every possible lead, no matter how insignificant it might seem.

As she reads through the file for the umpteenth time, she begins to feel a glimmer of hope. She knows that she is onto something and that she is a tad closer to solving the case than she had been before.

With her newfound sense of purpose, she makes a list of potential witnesses and makes a mental schedule to reach out to them in a particular order, determined to uncover the truth behind the mysterious murder of the young lady near the fashion magazine.

As she writes out a list of people to visit, Chase decides to start her investigation by visiting the body of the deceased lady at the morgue. Despite the fact that the autopsy results have already come in, she knows that there may be valuable clues that can only be discovered in person.

Walking through the sterile halls of the morgue, she can feel her heartbeat quicken with anticipation. The mystery of the lady's death hanging heavy in the air, and the determination to solve it no matter what mounting within her. The morgue attendant leads her to the cold storage room where the body is being kept. The room is dark and damp, and the smell of disinfectant hangs heavy in the air. The attendant opens the door to one of the metal drawers, revealing the body of the young woman who was found dead near the fashion magazine. She inhales deeply, bracing herself for what she just saw. The sight is gruesome, but she has to fight the urge to turn away. She is aware of how much she needs to stay strong and focused if she wants to uncover the truth behind the lady's death.

Chase spends the next few hours examining the body, taking detailed notes and photographs. Her eyes widen every time she looks at the body. The young lady looks so small and vulnerable lying there, with her long blonde hair spread out on the metal table. She feels a pang of sadness and anger at the thought of someone taking another person's life. Not minding the grotesque nature of her task, she allows her mind revel the thought of how each new piece of evidence brings her one step closer to solving the mystery. The investigation is going to pose a challenge; a challenge she is up for.

Finally, she prepares to leave the morgue, gathering her things and letting out a deep breath. This investigation will be her greatest confrontation yet, but she is eager to face it head-on. With her mind focused and her senses heightened, Chase is prepared to follow the clues and uncover the truth behind the incomprehensible death of the lady near the fashion store.

As she gets to her car, she sits for a moment, taking in everything she has seen and heard so far. The thought of the long way she has to go before she can solve the case threatens to overwhelm her, but she feels a glimmer of hope that she is on the right track. Chase drives back to the office, determined to keep working until she finds the person responsible for the young lady's death.

Walking to her office, she stops to exchange a few words of pleasantries with her coworkers who had introduced themselves earlier. She is excited to make new friends, hence the warmth and friendliness in her bearing. She smiles good-naturedly, saying hellos when ever she walks through their cubicles.

As she gets to her office, she is goes through the evidence she has been able to gather, and gives herself a mental tap on the back for putting in the effort. She proceeds to go through her list of people she is to interview and begins by calling the first person by the number provided in the file.

Chase catches herself thinking about the body she had seen at the morgue earlier, and is overcome by a feeling of bleakness. The image remains perfectly etched in her mind and questions keep springing from the emotional parts of her.

Was it slow and painful?

Was it quick and painless?

She tries to shake it out of her head but none of the distraction techniques she deploys work, leaving her frustrated and sad.

Second-guessing her entire life decisions are the next thing that comes to her mind, and they have never proved to be a good distraction because they only left her depressed with feelings of inadequacy.

Moreover, the last thing she wants to do now is let her brain trick her into believing she is not fit for her new promotion or job. It will only leave her devastated and unable to function properly.

Her superiors have too much faith in her, and having this mind-bogging responsibility to prove to her coworkers and superiors that she is fit for the new position conferred on her, and to ensure that justice is served for the young lady she saw at the morgue poking her being, she cannot allow negative self perception weigh her down.

She concludes it is in the best interest of herself and her work to leave and find something to eat.

Chase steps out her office and walks her way out of the office building, her eyes squinting in the bright sunlight. She takes a deep breath, inhaling the fresh air and trying to clear her mind of the overwhelming feeling that has been gnawing at her for hours. The murder case she is overseeing is a tough one, and it is beginning to consume her emotionally. Letting that happen would be highly inappropriate and unprofessional. She needs to take a break, even if it is just for a quick, late lunch.

As she walks towards the nearest lunch spot, her stomach growls loudly. Chase is a foodie at heart, and nothing can lift her spirits like a good meal. She has always believed that good food can heal even the most troubled mind, and today she needs that more than ever. The aroma of grilled chicken and freshly baked bread wafts through the air, drawing her towards the small deli on the corner. She has been too busy with work to remember how hungry she feels.

Entering the deli, Chase scans the menu, her eyes darting from one item to the next. Her mouth waters at the sight of the hot pastrami sandwich, but in the end, she settles on a turkey club. She orders her sandwich and a side of fries, then finds a table in the corner of the room. As she waits for her food, Rachel closes her eyes and takes a deep breath. The familiar smells of the deli and the chatter of the lunch crowd ease her mind, at least for the moment.

While Chase is enjoying her hot pastrami sandwich, she hears a familiar voice behind her. "Mind if we join you?" asks a voice.

She turns around to see two of her coworkers, Detective Johnson and Officer Jasmine, standing behind her with plates of their own.

"Please, sit," Chase replies, motioning to the chairs across from her. "I didn't expect to see you both here," she continues as they take their seats.

Detective Johnson chuckles.

"Well, it's not every day we get a chance to get out of the office and grab a bite to eat," he says. "Plus, the food here is pretty good."

Officer Jasmine nods in agreement, her mouth full of a juicy burger.

Chase smiles, happy to see them both. "Yeah, I'm considering coming here pretty often myself. It's a nice break from the daily grind."

They chat for a few minutes about work and what they have going on in their various departments, but soon the conversation turns to other topics, and before they know it, their lunch breaks are over, and it's time to head back to the office.

As they stand up, Detective Johnson turns to Chase. "Hey, thanks for letting us sit with you. It's good to take a break from the work and just hang out."

Chase nods. "Yeah, no problem. We should do it again sometime."

They say their goodbyes and they go their way, but Chase feels a little better than she did before. It's nice to have some company during her lunch break and to be reminded that she isn't alone in the ongoing struggle with these investigations.

After bidding her coworkers a quick goodbye, Chase finishes her fries and gathers her things, preparing to head back to the office. As she stands up, she hears her phone beep. A new email has just arrived in her inbox, from an unknown sender. She furrows her brow, puzzled. She doesn't recognize the email address, and the subject line reads simply "Important Information." Curiosity getting the better of her, she opens the email.

Inside, there is a short message, with no signature or identifying information. It reads: "For cool brew, come offer or we'll bunk." She reads it a few times and finally settles for reading it out loud, trying to make sense of it. Who could have sent it? Is it just a prank, or is there something more to it?

She looks around the deli, but can't see anyone suspicious. Detective Johnson and Officer Jasmine have already left, so she can't ask for their opinion. She decides to head back to the office and investigate the email further. As she walks back, she keeps a lookout for anyone following her, but the streets are quiet and empty.

When she reaches the office, she immediately goes to her desk and pulls up the email again. She runs a search on the sender's address, but it doesn't yield any results. She tries tracing the IP address, but it is masked by multiple proxies. The more she tries to find out, the more frustrated she becomes.

As she sits at her desk, contemplating the mysterious email, she begins to suspect that someone has been watching her. She looks up and scans the office, but everyone seems to be engrossed in their own work. She tries to push the thought away, but it lingers in her mind like a nagging feeling. What is the email about, and who has sent it?

Chase stares at the cryptic message on her screen, growing increasingly frustrated. She tries a few more online tools to decrypt the message, but they all prove to be useless. She even tries contacting a few friends who are skilled in cybersecurity, but they are all unavailable. It seems like every lead she tries to follow just leads to a dead end.

Just as she is about to give up and call it a day, a colleague walks into the office. He introduces himself as David, a new hire who has just joined the department. He is friendly and seems eager to get to know everyone. Chase welcomes him and they begin chatting about work.

As they speak, Chase realizes that it has gotten quite late. She checks her watch and is surprised to see that it is already past 6 pm. She has lost track of time completely while trying to decipher the mysterious email.

David notices her checking her watch and asks, "Are you not ready to go yet?"

Chase shakes her head, still a bit dazed. "No, I got caught up in something," she replies. "I need to finish up a few things before I can leave."

David nods understandingly. "Ah, I know how that goes," he says. "I'm just getting used to the workload myself. It's a lot to take in."

Chase smiles, feeling a little better. It's nice to talk to someone who is going through the same thing she is.

As David leaves to finish up his own work, Chase goes all out to refocus her attention on the investigation, and at the same time trying to shake off the strange feeling that has been lingering since she received the email, but it will not stop nagging at the back of her mind. She knows that she needs to figure out what the message means and who sent it. But for now, she has to focus on finishing up her work so she can head home and get some rest.

Soon, it dawned on her that she cannot concentrate anymore, so she goes ahead to clear her desk and shut down her computer, feeling a sense of relief that she can finally leave the office for the day. She gathers her belongings, grabs her coat, and heads out the door. As she walks to her car, she can't shake the feeling that something is off. She feels on edge, like someone is watching her every move.

Once she gets into her car, she takes a deep breath and tries to clear her mind. She starts the engine and begins the drive home, but her mind is preoccupied with the events of the day. She can't shake the memory of the murder she is investigating, the overwhelming feeling of sadness that has engulfed her, and the mysterious email that has left her feeling on edge.

As she drives down the deserted streets, Chase can't help but feel like she is being followed. She checks her rearview mirror multiple times but sees no one behind her. She knows it's probably just her imagination, but the feeling that something is not right is still lurking.

After a while, she arrives home and parks her car in the garage. She sits in the driver's seat for a moment, taking deep breaths to calm her racing heart. She knows she needs to shake off the feeling of unease that has been plaguing her all day, but it's easier said than done.

Right after she feels a little more composed, Chase gets out of her car and makes her way inside. She kicks off her shoes and collapses onto the couch, letting out a deep sigh. It's been a long and exhausting day, and she's grateful to be home at last. However, even as she tries to relax, her mind keeps returning to the events of the day. Bearing in mind that she might have a lot to process and a lot of work to do to unravel the mystery of the email, she decides not to let it distract her from the mission she has at hand.

Good morning, Chase!" David says as he looks up from the files he's trying to arrange on his table and sees Chase coming in. He hands her a cup of coffee, with a warm smile.

"Thank you so much, David," she replies, taking a sip of her coffee. "It's much needed today."

"You're telling me," David says, "I barely got any sleep last night. This job is really getting to me."

Chase knows exactly what he means. The murder investigation she is working on has been difficult, and it is starting to take a toll on her, and just like her, they all have their cross.

"I know how you feel," she says sympathetically. "But we have to keep pushing through. Hopefully, we'll be able to get the work done."

David nods in agreement. "You're right. We can't give up now."

As Chase walks over to her office to settle in, she feels an unwavering resolve. She has a lot of work to do, but with the support of her coworkers, she feels confident that she is not alone. She takes another sip of her coffee and gets to work, determined to make progress on the case.

Chase quickly gets to work, piecing together the events leading up to the victim's murder. She checks her list of people to interview, and decides to call Emily, the intern who had been the last person to speak with the victim. As she dials the number, she waits patiently for Emily to pick up on the other end.

Upon answering the call, Emily is unnerved by the news that she is being questioned in regards to the murder of a woman at the fashion store. Chase introduces herself and assures Emily that she is here to help and get to the bottom of what happened. Emily agrees to meet with Chase to discuss the matter further.

Chase immediately makes her way to the fashion store, where Emily has agreed to meet her after her shift. Upon entering the store, Chase feels the eyes of the employees upon her, likely wondering why a detective is present. She approaches the front desk and asks to speak with Emily, explaining that it is related to an ongoing investigation. After a brief wait, Emily appears, looking nervous and hesitant to speak.

Chase approaches Emily in a gentle manner, trying to put her at ease. She assures Emily that she is not a suspect and is only looking for information. Emily, still shaken, opens up to Chase and tells her everything she knows about the victim's final moments.

Chase pulls out her notebook and pen, taking notes as Emily speaks. She asks questions, hoping to gather any information that could potentially crack the case. Despite Emily's initial hesitation, she is able to provide valuable information.

Once she has all the information she needs, she thanks Emily for her time and assures her that she will do everything in her power to solve the case and bring justice for the victim.

Chase's curiosity gets the best of her after speaking with Emily, and she decides to take a brief tour of the fashion magazine to get a sense of the environment and possibly find any clues that could be relevant to the case.

She begins walking around the store, taking note of the various departments and scanning the employees who are going about their business.

As she walks, she notices that the magazine is quite busy, with customers bustling in and out of the various departments. She observes the different displays of clothes and the neatly arranged shelves that hold different accessories, all at the right place, not forgetting to note how well it is designed to be aesthetically pleasing and functional, making it easy for customers to browse and find what they need.

Also, she notices how the magazine is divided into different sections catering to various styles and trends, ranging from high-end fashion to more affordable options. Moving through the various sections, she takes mental and physical notes of everything she sees, with a strong determination to gather any information that could aid in the investigation.

Couture Chronicles is located on the outskirts of town, nestled in a secluded area surrounded by a dense forest. The driveway leading up to the magazine is long and winding, with tall trees towering over it, casting deep shadows that move and shift with the wind.

The magazine sits at the end of the driveway, with no other structures nearby. It's an eerie and desolate environment, with the building standing alone against a backdrop of trees and greenery.

The magazine itself is an old-fashioned building, with classic architecture that seems out of place in the modern world. The façade is made of smooth, time-worn stone, giving it a rustic charm. Large windows on either side of the entrance are framed with intricate wrought iron, and the door is heavy wood that creaks when opened.

Inside, it is as luxurious as its name suggests. Soft cream walls and polished marble floors provide the backdrop for the neatly arranged racks and shelves. Expensive perfumes and colognes scent the air while soft music plays in the background, creating an atmosphere of indulgence.

But despite the beauty of the magazine, an underlying sense of foreboding permeates the environment. The secluded location, winding driveway with blind spots, and eerie shadows dancing in the darkness create an atmosphere of danger. It's a place where one can easily forget the lurking dangers beyond the shadows.

Chase walks into the lobby of Couture Chronicles, the high-end fashion magazine, her eyes scanning the room for anything that can aid her investigation as she continues her tour, she cannot refrain herself from overhearing a heated conversation taking place in a nearby office. Curiosity gets the best of her, and she approaches the door, knocking lightly.

"Excuse me, is everything okay?" she asks, peeking inside.

Sitting at the desk is a woman who is clearly in distress, her face twisted in frustration.

The woman looks up, her eyes tired and worn. "No, everything is not okay," she sighs. "We've just received word that one of our photographers has cancelled last minute for our upcoming shoot, and we have no backup plan."

Chase nods sympathetically, recognizing the frustration of last-minute changes. "I'm sorry to hear that. Is there anything I can do to help?"

The woman looks at her quizzically before realizing who she is. "Oh, you must be the detective investigating the case outside. I'm Shiri Welles, the CEO of Couture Chronicles. Do you have any experience with photography?"

Chase raises an eyebrow, not quite sure where this is leading. "A little bit. Why?"

"Well, we could really use a fresh perspective on this. Would you mind taking a look at our mood board and giving us some ideas?" Shiri asks, leading Chase to the conference room.

As Chase flips through the pages of the mood board, she feels a pang of nostalgia for her own childhood dreams of becoming a fashion designer. "I like this color scheme," she says, pointing to a page with various shades of blue and green. "And have you considered shooting in an outdoor location?"

Shiri's eyes light up with excitement. "Those are both great ideas! Thank you so much for your help. Maybe we should hire you as a creative consultant," she jokes, her face breaking into a smile.

Chase chuckles, enjoying the change of pace from her usual crime-solving routine. "Maybe you should. But for now, I have a murder to solve."

Chase smiles, feeling a sense of accomplishment. Even though it isn't related to the murder investigation she's working on, she's glad to have been of assistance to Shiri and her business.

Shiri looks at her, suddenly realizing how one-sided and improper the introduction was and asks, "Excuse me, I didn't catch your name. Who are you?"

"I'm Chase, a detective with the local police department. I'm here to investigate the recent murder that occurred in the store," Chase replies, with a polite smile plastered across her face.

Shiri's expression turns serious as she realizes the reason for Chase's presence in her store.

"Oh, I see. Well, anything I can do to help, I will."

Chase thanks her and begins to ask Shiri a few questions about the murder, but she interrupts her. "I'm sorry, before we go any further, I need to know if there's anything I should be worried about. Is there any reason why the police would suspect me or anyone in my store?"

Without hesitation, Chase assures her that there is no reason to worry, but that she is just trying to gather information about the victim and the events leading up to their death.

Shiri nods, still looking concerned. "Okay, I understand. Please let me know if there's anything I can do to help with the investigation."

Chase thanks her again and takes note of Shiri's willingness to cooperate, bearing in mind that gaining the trust and cooperation of the people involved in the case will be crucial to solving it.

"Not bothering to check the time, Chase readily followed Shiri back to her office where they had been few minutes ago.

This time, the walked back with a different aura hanging between them, but she had resolved the spend her entire day there if need be.

She takes a seat in front of Shiri's desk and begins her interview. While at it, she occasionally got carried away by the CEO's striking beauty and captivating smile. The two women exchange glances and a subtle flirtation begins to develop between them.

In the course of answering the questions, Shiri explains that the victim was a shareholder in the magazine and also a very friendly and generous young woman without any trouble. Chase takes note of this information and continues to ask more questions about the victim's relationship with the magazine and its employees.

Shiri opens her mouth to speak but the she feels tears stinging in her eyes, and pauses, trying not to cry. She is making a serious attempt to keep her composure but the emotion is too much for her to bear.

She breaks into sobs. "I'm so sorry," she says after crying for a few minutes. "This is embarrassing. I'm so sorry."

Chase watches her helplessly, not knowing what to do to help her. She responds with a nod and a sad smile. "I can go and come back another time, you know," she says, hoping that might help. "I had no intention of interviewing you today, after all."

"No," Shiri says, shaking her head vehemently. "Let's continue this. I don't mind you coming around again when the original time you scheduled me for arrives."

As the interview continues, they find themselves laughing at each other's jokes and enjoying each other's company. Irrespective of the seriousness of the murder investigation, they can't help but be drawn to each other.

Shiri mentions that the victim was a regular customer who always came into the magazine to look at our designs and was well-liked by the staff because of how kind she was. She goes ahead to narrate how she began drawn to the magazine and the workers that she made her intentions of owning a share in the business as a way of showing her support.

Chase asks Shiri if she suspects anyone in the magazine had a serious problem with the victim that could have led to harming her, but Shiri cannot think of anyone who would have wanted to hurt the victim.

As the interview winds down, Chase thanks Shiri for her time and being helpful. She promises to stop by again for further questioning on account of her original interview schedule. Shiri smiles and tells her that she is happy and willing to do anything to assist with the investigation because a dear friend's life is at stake.

Chase stands up to leave, and Shiri walks her to the door. As they exchange a brief goodbye, they share a lingering glance and a subtle touch of the hand. They both withdraw with speed, as though trying to separate themselves from an electrifying surface. Despite the gravity of the situation, the chemistry between them is palpable.

With an elevated sense of intrigue and excitement, Chase walks away from the interview, knowing that she needs to focus on the investigation. Yet, she cannot stop herself from replaying what had happened back in Shiri's office. Is there a chance that Shiri shares even the slightest bit of chemistry with her?

Chase sits in her car for a few minutes, her mind racing with thoughts of what just happened between her and Shiri. She can't rid herself of the feeling that there is something between them, something more than just a professional connection. She replays the brief moment of physical contact a number of times in her mind, hoping to get the same feel as she did when the touch of Shiri's hand sent a shiver down her spine.

Her drive back to the office is preoccupied with the awareness of excitement mixed with uncertainty brewing in her. The investigation into the murder is already challenging, but now with the added complication of her feelings towards Shiri, it is going to be even more difficult to remain focused.

Her good records are not just any record, they are merited because how consistent she is at compartmentalizing her emotions, separating her personal life from her work life. However, something about Shiri is promising to make the task more challenging than usual. Chase can't deny the attraction she feels towards Shiri, but she also knows that the investigation has to take priority. She doesn't know how yet, but she knows something has to be done by her or the investigation will be tampered with.

As she navigates the streets towards the office, Chase tries to push her thoughts of Shiri aside and focus on the task at hand. She needs to review the evidence collected so far and see if there are any leads that could point them towards a suspect.

Despite her efforts to remain focused, Chase can't help but smile as she thinks about Shiri. The cobble wobbles she is experiencing are a welcome distraction from the difficult work ahead, even if they are also a source of uncertainty.

In no time, her car turns into the driveway of the office building, and she slows down as she approaches the parking lot. She maneuvers the car into an empty parking space and takes a deep breath before turning off the engine. She sits there for a moment, gathering her thoughts, trying to clear her mind of any distractions before stepping out of the car.

As she steps out of the car, the cool breeze hits her face as she pulls her jacket closer, and walking towards the entrance of her office building. She pushes the door slowly, not sure of what to expect.

To her surprise, the entire space is empty. Then, it comes to her mind what time it is and how everyone must have gone out in search of clues to one case or another just like she had done. She exhales deeply, squeezing her eyes shut.

"Chase?" Paul calls out, suddenly appearing from under one of the tables. "Good afternoon, Chase," he greets her with a note of glee, flashing his winning smile.

Chase stares at him amiss, trying to understand how he appeared out of the blue to occupy a space that was vacant only a few minutes ago.

"It's not what you think," he assures her with a giggle. "I managed to knock off a well-arranged pile of files and they flew everywhere, so I had to duck away to wriggle out of the mess I created."

"What do you mean 'wriggle out the mess I created'?" she asks, arching her eyebrows to create her signature questioning look.

"Just so you know, Chase," he says, fighting a laugh. "I am very heavy on taking responsibility."

It is Chase's turn to muffle a laugh except that she can't, so he joins her. She goes ahead to ask about the others, and he confirms her earlier thoughts before she heads to her office to get things done.

In her office, Chase busies herself with the notes she has collected so far without intrusive thoughts or sad emotions. She is just like her usual self at work. Suddenly, her phone chimes as an indication that she has received a notification and she rally to know what it is only to find another strange email sitting in her inbox. This time, the subject line reads "Last Warning." It is not the same subject but she feels the same feeling creeping unto her again as a shiver runs down her spine, triggering the eerie feeling she had before. She wonders if this is a prank or a real threat; something she should worry about.

With trembling hands, she opens the email and reads the message. The content is even more unsettling than the subject line. It reads "Bookcase nodded, deathly scoot."

Chase quickly scans the email again and again, trying to trace a pattern that could help her identify the sender. However, the email is written in the way the first one had been written. She feels helpless and vulnerable, once again, wondering if someone is watching her every move.

She knows she has to take action. But she archives the email, not ready to suspend her investigation for it. She notes to forward it to the IT department to see if they can trace its origin. She is afraid that the sender might have access to sensitive information that could compromise the investigation.

Over the next few hours, she tries to push the thought of the email out of her mind and focus on the work at hand. She has to review the evidence collected so far and see if there are any leads that could point them towards a suspect. However, she finds it difficult to concentrate, knowing that someone out there is watching her every move.

Letting her gaze travel around the office, she cannot help but wonder if the sender is someone she knows. Is it a colleague or someone from her past? She knows she has to be careful and keep her guard up. The murder investigation is already challenging enough, and now with the added stress of the unknown sender, it is going to be even more difficult to remain focused.

Chase ignores the strange email and focuses on her workload with determination, eager to unravel the mystery. She picks up her phone as soon as she enters her office and dials Shiri's number to schedule an appointment for the afternoon. Then, she goes to retrieve the deceased's background check report, which has been delayed due to technical issues in the forensics database.

To her surprise, she discovers that the deceased is Elizabeth Anne Coleman, who had only identified herself as Anne Ray at the fashion store. It becomes clear that she must have hidden her true identity to protect herself, but now her efforts have been in vain.

Elizabeth inherited a lot of wealth from her parents who were well-known socialites, but she didn't want to identify with it because of the danger it posed to her life. Her parents have made many enemies, and their wealth and status made her a target for jealousy and resentment which would come in the way of the simple life she wanted to live without any added stress or fear.

This made her deploy every tactic in the bid to distance herself from her family's name and fortune by living a modest lifestyle, only for her find that it was not always easy. People recognized her name and treated her differently, and she feared for her safety. She began to realize that no matter how hard she tried, she will never be able to completely separate herself from her family's legacy.

In an effort to protect herself and the fortune she was left with, Elizabeth decided to hire a team of security experts who can help her maintain a low profile and protect her from potential threats. They advised her to be cautious about who she trusted and to avoid drawing attention to herself. She followed their advice, but none of the enemies were willing to let her live.

At exactly 1pm, Chase is already at the fashion store, ready to interview Shiri again, as well as let her in on the recent discovery about Anne.

They go ahead to chat and have a few minutes conversation outside the main reason she came, after they exchange pleasantries.

Shiri breaks down to sobs again upon hearing about Elizabeth.

"That's really saddening," she says thoughtfully. "She knew her life was not safe and yet she was that kind and generous with us around here."

Chase agrees with her, knowing that herself was only able to not cry because of how much time she had taken to train her facial muscles.

The mere thought of a fellow human being living her while life in fear; fear of it being snuffed out of her at any time makes her want to cry, but how would that help Elizabeth? It would only make her lose time for the investigation, hence leaving the perpetrators an ample amount of time to disappear.

"Do you want us to take a break?" Chase asks thoughtfully, following how Shiri has grown tongue-tied over the passing minutes.

"No, I'm fine," she says. "Just that processing the whole thing because we were so close but she didn't even let me in on this because of how scared she was."

"Do not take it personal," Chase responds. "It is sad that even what's left of her relatives have no idea that she is deceased."

"You still have her body?" Shiri asks, looking alarmed and Chase responds with a nod.

After the several minutes spent on emotions, Chase decides to try the next thing on her last St which was profiling and running a background check on every single one of the staff at Couture Chronicles.

At first, Shiri is resistant, not knowing how that is going to take a toll on her business, but Chase is able to talk her into it.

"Sweetie," Chase calls, letting her catch a glimpse of the fire burning in her eyes by lifting her face by the chin and staring into her eyes passionately. "Tell me, how much support are you willing to give to make sure your shareholder gets justice?"

Chase can sense her delay, so she wants to know how ready she is to support her with the investigation.

After a few minutes of thinking, she nods and hands her a flash that contains the complete database.

"Will you keep me posted?" She asks as Chase is about to leave.

"Do you want me to?" Chase asks.

"Yes, please," she responds.

"Then consider it done, sweetie," she says with a smile. "We're partners in this investigation now."

They say their goodbyes and Chase heads back for the office.

Shiri spends the next several minutes after Chase leaves, thinking about her. There's something about her and how she makes her feel that she can't quite put her finger on. It isn't just the way Chase looks, although she's undeniably attractive. It's the way she carries herself with such confidence and authority. Shiri has always been drawn to strong, independent women, and Chase is definitely one of them.

As she stands there, lost in thought, she can't help but wonder if Chase feels the same way. Does she sense the attraction between them? Or is she so focused on the investigation that she doesn't even notice?

Shiri shakes her head, trying to clear her thoughts. She can't afford to get distracted now. There's a killer on the loose, and they need to be caught before they strike again. As much as she's drawn to Chase, she knows that the investigation has to come first.

But as the days go by, she finds it harder and harder to keep her mind off of Chase. Every time she sees her, she feels a flutter in her stomach, and she can't help but wonder what it would be like to kiss her. It's a dangerous thought, one that she knows could lead to trouble, but she can't help herself.

After weeks of fruitless attempts to ignore her feelings, Shiri decides to take a chance. She calls Chase that evening to ask about her progress with the investigation and files she collected earlier.

"It's going well, Sweetie," Chase answers mindlessly, certain that there's more to the call than what she's letting on. "Tell me, how have you been?"

"I'm trying to stay afloat," she responds. "You know a lot is happening at the same time."

"Yeah," Chase agrees. "But I hope you understand that you're prior, and you shouldn't let it affect you that much."

Shiri nods in agreement from her end as if Chase is there with her.

"I was going to ask if you're going to be chanced sometime this week," she says with a drag. "I would like us to have dinner together."

"Oh, wow!" Chase exclaims out of feigned surprise. "I would love that too."

Despite the relief that floods over her, Shiri still can't shake the feeling that there's something between them. She's tried to deny it for so long, but it's become impossible to ignore. She wonders if Chase feels it too, or if she's just imagining things. Either way, she's willing to take a chance.

At the office, Chase pursues the investigation with heightened vigor and energy, blocking off every form of distraction that tries to present itself.

To take the investigation to the next level, Chase decided to send the files of all the staff at Couture Chronicles which she got from Shiri to the IT department for profiling and background checks. She knew that this was a necessary step in the investigation, but also understood that it could create tension between the police and the store's employees.

Despite the potential backlash, Chase believed that it was important to follow all leads and leave no stone unturned. She had a strong sense of justice and a desire to protect her community, and was willing to take whatever steps were necessary to solve the case.

The IT department worked quietly, making sure to avoid raising any red flags. The profiling and background checks are being conducted discreetly, so as not to tip off any potential suspects. Chase had emphasized the need for secrecy, knowing that the culprit could be anyone, even one of their own.

She watches from a distance, monitoring their progress, making sure that everything is done with utmost care and meticulousness. The investigation is reaching a critical stage, and any misstep could jeopardize everything they've worked so hard for.

As the hours tick by, she can't help but feel a sense of unease, a nagging feeling that something isn't quite right. She trusts her team, but there's always the possibility of a mole, someone who's working against them from the inside.

Chase is determined to finish the task before leaving, but she realizes that her early dinner with Shiri is approaching. She speaks with one of the officers in the department and informs him that she will be back in the next hour or so, making him promise that the task will be completed before she returns, and she thanks him before rushing out of the office.

As she drives to the restaurant where she and Shiri agreed to meet, she can't help but feel a sense of excitement mixed with nervousness. She's been looking forward to this dinner for days, and now that it's finally happening, she can't help but wonder what it means. Is this just a friendly dinner between friends, or is there something more between them?

Chase shakes her head, trying to clear her thoughts. She knows that she needs to stay focused on the task at hand, but her mind keeps drifting back to Shiri. There's something about her that she cannot get herself to ignore, and for that reason, she is drawn to her in a way that she's never felt before.

As she arrives at the restaurant, she sees Shiri waiting for her at a table by the window. She smiles nervously as she approaches, unsure of what to say. But as soon as they start talking, she feels a sense of ease wash over her. They talk about the case, their work, and their personal lives, and as the evening wears on, she realizes that she has fallen so hard for Shiri.

But even as she feels herself getting closer to Shiri, she knows that she needs to stay focused on the investigation. The killer is still out there, and they're running out of time. As much as she wants to be with Shiri, she knows that she can't let her guard down just yet.

Heading back to the office, eager to receive the reports from the IT department, she receives another email as she fumbles with her car key. The subject, just like the other ones, is strange. It reads "Say Your Last Prayer." Without caring to know what the body has to say, she slides into her car and locks it from inside, because more than ever, the aura is thick with dread and gloom, and she can feel eyes piercing through her body.

Then, she sees a hazy figure appear from the dark driveway which has the same atmosphere and blind spots like the one at Couture Chronicles. She is too occupied with her date with Shiri that she didn't take any note of the strangeness.

Putting her car in drive, she turns as quickly as possible, missing it only by a few inches. A metal object which it was hiding in its sleeve falls out in the process. Suddenly, the figure steps away, disappearing into the shadows as quickly as it appeared. Chase drives without looking back, gasping for air, tears burning in her eyes as she hopes that Shiri is safe. She knows that she has been given a second chance, that she has escaped death by a hair's breadth, but the thought of what could have been sends shivers down her spine.

She dials Shiri's number, and Shiri picks up in an instant.

"Can you stay till I send someone to pick you up?" She asks, trying not to sound frantic.

"Yes, sure," she responds, unsure. "Did something happen?"

"Not really," she says. "I'm sending the person now."

She walks into her office building with her heart pounding in her ears. She walks directly to the IT department and retrieves the files, skimming through them there and then.

"This guy," she says pointing a particular staff whose profile is almost bare. "He's a Digital Media intern, and he looks nothing 23. Run this blurry passport through all the databases, now."

The guy in charge takes the file back from her and gets to work, wondering what came over her.

Chase walks into her office and takes off her jacket and sends for Paul.

"Can you send someone to go pick Shiri Welles at Emerald Room, not very far from here."

"You got it," he says, not bothering to ask questions.

At the same moment the IT genius calls her attention to the real profile of the Digital Media intern, revealing that he is a 31-year-old two-time ex-convict who is about to become a third-time convict Shiri walks up to her, and they grab each other in a hug. Just then, she is informed that her superior is calling for her in his office. She drops her phone and rambles about the strange emails she had been receiving, before hurrying off to give a report of what happened not too long ago.

"You were attacked?" can be heard from the superior's office, and everyone comes to a halt, creating pin-drop silence. Immediately, Chase and Lieutenant Alvarez storm out of the office to announce that everyone is now involved in the investigation since Detective Chase's life is in danger.

They all get to work, searching for the supposed Digital Media Intern and the last place he was seen. In a matter of minutes, he is on his way to the Phoenix Gateway Airport to catch the 9:30 PM flight to Montreal.

A call Is placed to the airport, and they are to seize him immediately when they see him. Chase, Johnson, and two officers hurry to the airport to seize him. It is about a 30-minute drive.

The IT genius shouts, "Anagrams!" and walks over to Chase, handing her the phone.

"What do they mean?" She asks, surprised at her inability to decipher the email.

"The first one is 'For cool brew, come offer or we'll bunk' which translates to 'Back off or we'll come for you,' and the second one 'Bookcase nodded, deathly scoot' translates to 'Don't do this to yourself, Chase. Back down.' While the last one 'As a Dreamy Ode, Duet' is 'You're a deadmeat.'"

"Wow," Chase says quietly. "Well, thank you."

She hurries out after the others to apprehend the intern.

Successfully, they bring him in, and with the new interrogation techniques tailored to each suspect, they drill the truth out of him in no time.

He mentions the names of the people behind the death, confessing that he joined the fashion magazine because of the victim's affiliation with them.

Chase takes his cooperation into account and ensures with every courage and strength her being could summon that the real perpetrators are sentenced for their evil doings.

• • •

Chase sits at her desk in her office, watching the news on her computer screen. It's a sunny afternoon, but the brightness of the day is in stark contrast to the somber mood that hangs in the air. The news anchor is reporting on the sentencing of the two socialites behind the death of Elizabeth Anne Coleman, the young heiress whose life was cut short in a senseless act of envy and greed.

Chase's eyes are fixed on the screen, her expression unreadable. She feels a mix of emotions as she watches the news unfold. Relief that justice has been served, but also sadness that a young life was lost so needlessly. She thinks about the months she spent investigating the case, the evidence she gathered, and the emotional toll it took on her.

As the news segment ends, Chase leans back in her chair and lets out a long sigh. She feels a sense of closure, but also a deep sadness for the Coleman family and the loss they have suffered. She knows that justice can never truly bring back what was taken from them, but she hopes that it can at least bring them some measure of peace.

Later in the evening, Chase goes to the fashion magazine to pick up Shiri for their date, unannounced.

"Baby, you're here!" Shiri exclaims upon noticing her at the door. "How long have you been here?" "Long enough to know you've done enough work for today," she says pulling her closer by the waist, and leaning in to kiss her passionately.

Together, they leave the magazine, happy at the outcome of their efforts. As they drive to the restaurant, Chase narrates the whole celebration they pulled off for her at the office for the success of the investigation, and how her superior warned her never to keep everyone out of the loop like that again to avoid loss of life.

Shiri laughs at that, grabbing her right hand for a gentle squeeze.

"You didn't lose your life, baby. You didn't," she says, kissing the back of her hand.

The Priestess And The Pirate

Hala lay on the bed in her room. She had a stressful day overlooking the elven temple as the chief priestess. The job was very draining and she seemed to have lost all her energy.

She wanted to lie down and have a quiet evening but she felt so restless. She couldn't sleep a wink. She wanted to go outside alone and get some fresh air but as the elven priestess, she would not be allowed that luxury.

She rose from her bed, eager to do anything to get the fresh air she so desperately desired. She walked to the door of her room and peered out. The hallway seemed to be empty.

She quietly crept out of her room and down the hallway. She walked to the great library in the temple. She crept in without checking, she knew no one would be in there at this time.

She walked over to a bookshelf that seemed abandoned with cobwebs growing out of every book. She pulled each book looking for the secret entrance that she knew was there.

She pulled the last book on the shelf and the bookshelf pulled open. She walked down the twisting chairs that deposited her at the back of the temple, in a beautiful garden with views of the sea.

Almost no one knew about this place so Hala was going to get the relaxation she needed. She was breathing in the fresh air when a handkerchief was placed over her mouth and nose gagging her.

Hala woke up in a strange room. She tried to move and realized that her hands and legs were tied. The room seemed to be swaying. The only light in the room came from a window too far high for Hala to reach.

Hala looked around her and her eyes seemed on the figure in the corner of the room. The figure stepped out of the shadows when they saw that Hala had seen them, it was a female.

"Hello, I am Lena and you are aboard my ship ." The figure said.

"Please let me go. If you want treasure, my people will gladly offer a large amount of money for their priestess' life." Hala pleaded.

"I believe you but whatever your people might offer. The people who sent you to kidnap you will offer a lot more." Lena said a matter of factly.

"Please just release me, I will not tell anybody it was you."

"Get some rest," Lena said, before walking out of the room.

Hala was restless. She felt even worse than she did at the temple. She tried to sleep but everywhere was too uncomfortable for her. She pressed herself into a corner. Soon fatigue took over and she drifted off into a silent sleep.

Hala woke up to someone lightly shaking her. She opened her eyes to see Lena staring down at her with a guilty expression on her face.

"What do you want?" Hala hissed at her.

" I wanted to say I am sorry. I don't normally abduct people." Lena said, feeling a bit guilty.

Hala felt bad for her rude tone when she heard the remorse in Lena's voice. She looked at the woman next to her intently.

"Then why did you kidnap me?" Hala asked, breaking the silence that had grown between them.

"I need the money." Came Lena's silent reply.

"Take me home. My people with grant you tons of treasure." Hala insisted.

"Your offer sounds tempting but the amount of money I going to be given upon your delivery is beyond imagination. Without it, I can't leave this life."

"Leave this life?"

"Yes. I want to go as far as here from possible and start a new life with people who don't know who I am. A life where people don't have a fixed idea of me. I could choose a new name and be whoever I wanted to be and only their only money can get me that." Lena said.

They both sat in awkward silence. Lena wondered why she had told that to a stranger. I will never probably see her again she thought to comfort herself. She looked at Hala under the dim light.

She turned to leave the room when Gala's voice interrupted her.

"I understand," Hala said, causing Lena to look at her in confusion. How could an elven priestess understand her to need to be free?

"I love my job as the chief priestess but sometimes I feel it is a bit demanding. I never get the freedom to just do what I want. Everything I do is pre-planned and prepared for me so I understand." Hala continued.

Hala went back to her spot next to Hala. They sat next to each other in silence. They were both two peas in a pod, going through the same problem.

"Hey, can you untie so I can get some fresh air? I was in the middle of that when you kidnapped me." Hala said.

Lena thought about it and realized that she had no chance of escaping because they were surrounded by sea and the next island wasn't for miles.

"I promise I won't run." Hala insisted.

Lena have a nonchalant shrug and went to untie her. She loosened the knot holding her legs together. She started to work on the rope that bound her hands together.

She pulled it and with one tug it came loose. She stepped back and slip on the rope and fell on Hala. Their lips collided on impact. The air felt tense around them.

They both lay there frozen in shock. They both pressed their lips together, deepening the kiss. Lena pulled back and stared into Gala's eyes red-faced.

She got up from Hala and quickly left the room while she was still blushing. Hala stood up from the ground.

She was happy that she was free from her job as the chief priestess but most of all she was happy that she was going to start a new life with Lena.

Sisters

Lara Addams and Barbara Jones, two lesbian friends, had just gotten admitted into Calvary college, Fifty miles away from their hometown. Two weeks before their resumption, they began to gather things they would need in their new school without struggling to stress themselves in a new environment.

Before that, Lara sent numerous emails to the school to request the same hostel with her beautiful lover, Barbara. They were both so determined to stay in the same room, just the two of them since they could not afford the accommodation fees, and in order to have enough space and privacy to explore their bodies.

Knowing the school would hardly grant their requests, they both lied in the mail, telling the school they needed to stay together because they were sisters. Stating further, Lara claimed that Barbara is an asthmatic patient, which means the attention and care of a close relative.

A false Doctors report was attached to the mail, and luckily for them, their request was granted, thereby giving two old lovers a chance to love every night.

Lara met Barbara while in high school. She has always admired Barbara's determination and boldness, unlike herself – feeble and fearful. Barbara was the leader of the cheerleaders. Each time, she would secretly admire her ass cheeks, protruding and struggling to pop out of her shorts skirt. Lara has always fantasized about grabbing that cheeky backside and squeezing them lightly. But all she could do was imagine and just imagine. She was a freak everyone hated, and walking up to a cheerleader and telling her of her feelings would just ruin her reputation totally.

Rather, she decided to remain hidden and imagine things she could do while she wrote of Barbara in her journals. Barbara, on the other hand, has a soft spot for Lara. Anytime one of her close friends brings up Lara's case to mock her, and she always stands to defend her, no matter the circumstances. Lara and Barbara were both dreamers who were not bold enough to voice out their feelings and emotions.

Barbara's boldness could not help her in this situation since she did not want the whole to know that she was into girls. She keeps looking at her waistline when she is in class or walking by shyly.

They were both unaware of their helpless and hopeless situation until fate unexpectedly brought them together. Lara had run into the comfort of the lady's room to cry after a group of boys made fun of her incredibly short skirt and crop top.

She was sitting on the floor, crying out her eyes, when Barbara accidentally came in and locked the door behind her just to reapply her makeup and wear a pad for her monthly flow.

She was attracted by the muffled cry down the bathroom. She walked further and saw her crush, looking hot in her outfit, crying hard.

" Baby girl, why are you here, crying?" asked Barbara. Lara did not hear anyone coming closer to her as she sprang up, quickly almost losing her balance, but was caught by Barbara. They both felt slightly relaxed to be in each other's arms as they continued to stare. Lara quickly regained her posture and thanked Barbara.

" I was not crying. Just meditating," she lied.

" You are a pretty bad liar, you know? Your makeup is smeared," added Barbara.

" Yes. About that...I'm actually fine," replied Lara as she blushed hard and tried to cover her face.

" Come, let me help you with your makeup. You can't go out like this. Come here, sit," commanded Barbara as she took Lara's hand, leading her to the nearby chair in the bathroom.

As their hands touched, they could both feel the spark and connection between them. It was a feeling of belonging and love since they both desired each other desperately.

They both looked at each other and smiled without saying a word. Barbara helped Lara with her makeup, making silly and funny jokes as she did to make her feel relaxed. She felt moved and wet just by touching Lara so close as she applied the makeup. She trailed her eyes and hands a little in between her medium-sized breast, watching as her chest heaved up and down with her thrilling and gentle touch.

Barbara asked why she was crying again, and this time around, Lara opened up to her. Lara told her about the way the popular school bullies made fun of her straightened hair, makeup, and short skirt, which made her cry.

" You look hot and cute in this dress. I bet they were jealous of your transformation," encouraged Barbara.

" You think so? I feel like I look horrible" replied Lara.

" Come on, don't cry. You'll spool your makeup. Now, stand up and give me a spin," said Barbara. Lara was a little bit nervous as she stood and slot turned around. She signaled to her to turn around again and, this time, told her to bend a little. Lara did as instructed; she bent, and in full view, Barbara could see her very backside, inviting and rounded. She smacked her slightly and gave her a little squeeze.

Lara was surprised at the gesture and quickly turned back with a shocked expression.

" I'm sorry. I should not have done that. I did not know you don't like stuff like that," said Barbara.

" I'm, I'm not offended. I am just shocked that you are into that kind of stuff. I thought you have a boyfriend," she replied.

" No. I'm actually into you. Since I met you, I knew I could never have a boyfriend. I feel so attached and attracted to you," said Barbara.

" Really? You also do? I don't know how to talk to you. I fucking love you," said Lara.

" I never knew you had a thing for me. All I knew was that my heart skips a bit each time I see you, and I can not help it. All the time, I'm tempted to bite your lips and grab your backside as you walk. I was just not bold enough to tell you how I feel," said Barbara

"I am so glad we have this moment to ourselves. Every night, I keep imagining how I would do things to you to make you madly pleasured while you do things to me. I want you to be my girlfriend," Lara said as she held Barbara's hand and placed it on her breast, as she stared deep into her eyes.

Barbara squeezed her firm and soft breast as she smiled and, in an instant, locked lips with Lara. Lip locking has always been on their minds, with the way they kissed hungrily and moaned low into each other's mouths, trying not to attract the attention of other students.

Barbara found Lara's center and touched it, feeling the lightly sticky liquid on her panties. She rubbed her slowly and gently as she continued to kiss her.

" wait. We can not do this here" chipped in Lara.

" you are right. If we get caught, we will be in great problem. We need to be discreet in all we do," added Barbara.

" The world will not accept us for who we are. What are we going to do? Will our love just end?" asked a confused and sad Lara.

" No. Our love will grow. Nothing and no one can stop us. We will just make it secret. My parents will be out of two for two days this weekend. Can you come over to my place? We'll have the whole place to ourselves," suggested Barbara.

" I think I can tell my parents that I'm coming to study at your place. Luckily, we stay in the same neighborhood; they know your parent. I'm sure they won't disagree" she said.

" Alright. I can't wait to have you. I will see you at night, okay?" said Barbara as she hugged Lara right and kissed her lips deeply before leaving the bathroom.

That day, Lara was chanced to visit Barbara at her home for a sleepover. Without her parent knowing what she was up to, they gave her permission to go and stay overnight. The love birds were both excited when they were finally chanced to be alone and do whatever they want to do. After properly securing the door, Barbara welcomed Lara with a deep kiss.

Lara sucked on Barbara's lower lips, tugging her hands firmly in her kinky full hair, pulling Barbara in deeper for a lovers' kiss. At the same time, Barbara moaned into her mouth, with her hands surveying every corner of her slender body.

After a while, they both made their way to Barbara's room and lay on the bed, kissing. Lara's hands traced Barbara's body, taking in every single detail. Lara gently held her neck, running her slender fingers down her collarbone, noting that Barbara was more fleshy than her. As her hands reached her breast, she cupped the full and soft breast in her hands and pressed hard, making Barbara rub her lower parts more on her.

She discovered that where Barbara was full and curvy, like the hips, which were properly curved, resulting in a beautiful big backside, enough to fit her entire body. While her body was large, Lara's body was slender and easy to lift.

Barbara rolled Lara to her back and kissed her cheeks, down to her collarbone, her breast line, and the space between her breasts, kissing and sucking and leaving a red spot. She found the entrance between her parted legs, wet and hot. She placed her hand on Lara's throbbing clit, pinching it. Lara broke the kiss, as Barbara inserted her middle finger Into Lara's tight hole. Lara gasped at the sharp impact of her finger, making her grab the sheets off the bed.

Lara breathed heavily into Barbara's neck as she slowly and crazily moved in and out of her, about to swell cochie. Lara held her shoulders tightly, digging in her fingers as Barbara added a second finger. She managed to stiffen her moans which were gradually filling the entire room. The spark between them continued to glow as they were pleasured. Barbara increased the intensity of the electricity in her fingers, faster and harder.

By this time, Lara was already at the edge of the bed, with her body Vibrating like a shocked Human. Barbara tried to insert a third finger, but Lara flinched and let out a shrill silent cry.

" That hurts? Asked Barbara. I'm sorry, I didn't know you were still a virgin," she added.

" Yes, I'm still a Virgin. But, you can break me," replied Lara.

Barbara stood from the bed, went to her locker, and brought out a long rubber dick. She pressed a button, and it started vibrating vigorously in her hand. Lara opened her mouth to ask about its use but was shut up by a kiss. Slowly, Barbara brought it to her parted legs and placed it first on her swollen clit, making her opening move in great anticipation and haste. It Vibrated against her opening, which made her close her open legs.

Successfully, Barbara was able to get it into her with few difficulties. She bled a little after trying to force it into her and also felt some pain, but the vibrator, soon made her relax. In and out, circling and teasing, she thrust the vibrator. Lara had the best night, as she could not get enough. She wanted her to stop due to the pain and also continue due to pleasure.

Lara rolled her eyes as she felt the vibrator deep in her, moving shockingly, touching all her sensitive internal as she cum.

Ever since Barbara and Lara have been together and professing their love secretly without anyone suspecting to remain together, they chose to go to the same College but were encountered by a little problem.

As they could not afford accommodation outside campus, they had no other option than to take the school hostel. To keep their love secret and avoid capital punishment, they had to request the same room instead of different ones. Staying in the same room will give them all the needed privacy without suspicion from other roommates.

They were both able to conjure a beautiful lie and their request was granted based on the health challenges of Lara who posed as the younger sister. Their parents were not aware of their plans and frequent love affairs, as they never thought their children could be indulged in things like that.

On the day they were to leave, they both sat side by side on the train, touching and smiling. At a point, Barbara placed Lara's hand under her skirt while no one was watching. As she parted her legs for Lara, the rushing air hit her bare center as she sucked in a breath. Lara touched her unclad lower parts and realized that she was not with panties. Her hands were welcomed by a warm liquid, housed by her throbbing clit and warm joining.

Lara understood her message and winked at her, getting off her seat and heading to the bathroom. A few seconds later, she was joined by Barbara who hurriedly smacked her lips against hers, kissing her hard and sweet. Barbara was beyond hot and lustful. She sat on the toilet lid, with her legs opened wide and each placed against the wall.

Lara smiled and kissed her forehead, noticing her heaving and racing heart as she knelt in front of her, parting her inner lips with her hands to give her more access. Teasingly, she stretched her tongue and licked her from the back to her clit, making her shudder in great relief and pleasure.

They felt a bit comfortable on the train because no one would ever suspect two young ladies going to the toilet together to do something strange, unlike a man and woman. Assuming it was a young uncourt lady with a young man going to the toilet, people would raise their brows and grumble at their indecent behavior of having sex in a public train.

Lara took one part of her inner lips and sucked, drawing the strands of hair in her pubic area. Barbara clasped her hands tightly over her mouth to avoid letting out a loud moan. Lara paid more attention to her clit, licking, sucking, and biting. She opened her mouth wide, and sucked at her center, drawing a white liquid from her and taking it all in.

Barbara could not handle the tingling feeling she got in her stomach as Lara licked her clean in the tight toilet train on their way to school.

With her heart racing, picking up speed like a pumped-up and energized Private plane, she slid her eyes tight while her legs tried to close up. Her hand was deep in Lara's wavy brown hair, tugging at her, encouraging her not to stop and to fasten her pace. With her hand, she rhythmically moved Lara's head till she exploded in Lara's mouth all her milky liquid.

Her breaths returned to normal after their little ordeal. Lara cleaned her up, licking her up while she called down.

Like nothing happened, they both returned to their seats, smiling and giggling.

A few hours later, they were standing right outside their college gate, ready to start a wonderful life together, far from home. They successfully checked in to their hostel, but their little secret was soon exposed.

Before they unpacked, they made the mistake of not locking their door, out of excitement. They passionately kissed and fondled each other's breasts when the door opened. They were both shocked at the unexpected change in the event.

"When you ladies kept sending mail after mail, demanding to be together, I knew something was wrong," said a pretty tall blonde with heavy makeup and long lashes with properly trimmed long nails. They were both speechless as they kept staring at the intruder with a hot, amazing body.

" And you are?" asked Lara.

" The hall President, Elizabeth Meroy. You guys have an explanation to do". She said and shut the door behind her, bolting it.

" I'm sure you know it's proper to knock on the door, Elizabeth. It's not right to barge in on people while doing something serious and private," said Barbara.

" And we will appreciate it if you will just get out of our room and let us be," added Lara.

"I can't just let you be. Do you know what happens when you get caught? First, you will be expelled and then face the jury. Hold on, did you think you are together because of your silly emails to the school? Far from that, I made it happen," said Elizabeth.

"Okay. Fine. I'm sure you now know we are lovers. You caught us right in the act. And thanks for helping us get this space. So, what do you want from us?" asked Barbara

" Good. Now, you are just talking. What I want is not difficult. You only, you become my favorites; you disobey, you get expelled," she threatened.

" Just tell us what you want. Money?" asked Lara.

" All I want is to be part of this little fun you guys are having. It's difficult to get a partner around here. You guys are really lucky, and I'm jealous," said Elizabeth.

" You mean, you are a lesbian too?" asked Lara.

" To confirm your doubts, see this," said Elizabeth as she grabbed Barbara by the chin, propped her up, and kissed her hard on her cute lips.

Lara and Barbara thought of what to do before they came to a difficult but interesting solution.

Lara and Barbara were both speechless at what they had just heard. They could not believe anything they had just heard. They never imagined someone would come in between them this way. They both thought of what to do to get out of their mess.

"Can you imagine what that lady with slim waist was saying?" said Barbara

" It's actually disgusting. I can't share you with any tall or short lady with long lashes and green eyes. We need to think of another way to get rid of her. At least to get her off our backs. I can't share you with anyone," said Lara.

" We have no other option now. Do we? I mean, I can't share you with anyone too, but we need to help ourselves. And, she is not that bad, either," added Barbara.

" you have a point, there. She doesn't look bad at all. But does that mean we have to succumb to her wishes? I mean, we have to have to make love with her?" asked Lara

" I guess that is our option. We can not report her to the authorities, which will get us in trouble. And she also helped us get this room. And I can not deny the fact that her lips taste great. Without her, we will be apart, remember?" said Barbara

" She looks hot enough for us. So, do we have a deal? To make her one of us?" asked Lara, again to be sure of her decision. Barbara agreed to the deal and made their intentions known to Elizabeth.

Their decision made Elizabeth glad and excited.

" Oh, my God. I'm so glad you, babes, agreed. I've been looking forward to a day like this, with pretty ladies like you, duo.

It was a tough agreement for them as they never thought of sharing themselves with another person. When they were still in high school, Antonio, a Spanish guy, tried to woo Barbara because of her amazing and striking features. She turned down his request, but he kept pestering her with annoying attentions and silly gifts, which made Barbara angrier and angrier at him.

Barbara told Lara, who was very angry at Antonio, who was trying hard and mad to get her to be his girlfriend. Determined to get him out of their lives, they both made a plan to expose one of his darkest secrets to the whole school.

Antonio once assaulted a Junior student in the school, but he threatened the girl, so she could not voice out her pain. The girl he assaulted still walked the school grounds, but with great fear of Antonio. Antonio thought he got away with his crime, not knowing he would later meet his Waterloo.

Lara and Barbara leaked his secret and got Justice for the assaulted girl while Antonio was expelled from school.

Ever since the disappointment of Antonio, no one came into their lives until the appearance of Elizabeth.

Even though lesbianism was not an acceptable union in New York, then, people still found ways to secretly get engaged to their lovers. Police raids were conducted then to arrest those who were known to be gay lovers.

Lara and Barbara were lucky enough not to be caught by the police one fateful afternoon in the park. They were both sitting under a big tree, enjoying the breeze and cool shade. They were holding hands and softly massaging their legs.

They were both smiling and lost consciousness of their environment as they kissed themselves in public. It was at this moment that a police officer passed them by; he saw and caught them red-handed, but rather than take them to the police station, he took them to a nearby wood.

They were both ready to do anything to get out of the mess they were in. The officer ordered them to get on their knees in front of him.

" You bastard are extremely lucky today. Consider this your lucky day as I won't take you to the station where you will be judged. Now, all I need is your warm and cute lips around my shaft," he said.

It was a case of their reputation, and without thinking twice, they obeyed his every instruction. They both knelt in front of him, while Lara brings out his sleeping, curvy fat dick. Barbara took it in, in her warm mouth, sucking deep and long.

The officer moaned loud enough to scare the animals in the woods away, with his eyes shut, enjoying the pleasure he was getting from the ladies.

That was the only time the love birds could remember ever getting someone between them, and it was to save their reputation and life.

They took turns sucking on his fat dick before he shot rope after rope of his seed into their mouth.

After he left, Lara had to throw up after taking his smelly and stinky cum in her mouth. Since then, she swore never taken any more dick in her mouth.

Now, to deal with Elizabeth, all they had to think of a better way to help themselves instead of getting expelled and arrested. It took them a lot of decision and courage to allow a third party in their lives; after all they have been through since high school, till now when they are finally able to live together.

They came to a conclusion, to agree with Elizabeth and make her their third partner, just for the main time they are in College. The last thing they needed on their neck was the school authorities and government officials dragging them from court to court, with their parents totally disappointed in them.

After the agreement, they decided to meet later in the night to have pleasing and pleasant fun in their room with Elizabeth joining them.

After they agreed to the terms, Elizabeth left with the promise to come back in the night, to explore the sexuality of Lara and Barbara.

Barbara and Lara, could not arrange their things immediately, as they had to complete some other registration in the hostel. To avoid getting into trouble, they left their things to complete the formalities. After everything was done and ready, they went into town to get a few outfits for their new classes. They did some shopping and stopped by to eat at a roadside restaurant.

They both discussed about what was going to happen that night with Elizabeth as they ate.

" I strongly hope this won't be a long-term thing with her," commented Barbara

" Let us just hope she doesn't bother us too much with her desires," added Lara.

" We need to head back to the hostel now to clean out our room before it becomes dark," said Barbara.

" Don't you think we should get some small chops, you know, to keep our mouths busy?" suggested Lara.

" Come on, you have my mouth to keep you busy, Forget about chops," smiled Barbara.

They both went back to the hostel and tried to unpack when a knock was heard on their door. It was Elizabeth with her long lashes, dressed in short blue jeans and a top that barely covered her firm breast.

They allowed her on and shut the door behind her, locking it. Their room was still messy as they could not properly arrange it before her unannounced visit. She could not wait until 9 pm when we were sure everyone would have settled down and Probably be sleeping due to the stress of packing and unpacking.

Elizabeth could not hold on till night before she got into action. Right in the middle of the room, she stripped off her top, barely covering her big, firm breasts. Her erect nipples could be seen peeking out from the top she wore. She let go of the top, revealing her busty breasts, as Lara and Barbara looked on in anticipation.

Once the top was off her head, they both leaped forward and, like two hungry kids, took each of her breasts in their mouths, sucking with determination to get something out of her huge breast.

Elizabeth moaned in low tunes, letting out gasps at the interval as Lara's middle finger curled up into her, found the right spot, and continued to hit with her finger. She withdrew her finger and inserted three of her fingers all at once into Elizabeth while Barbara bit her nipple hard.

She Let out a yelp from the result of the pleasure before suppressing her moans. They landed on the bed and repositioned themselves. Lara lay on the bed, with her back, with Barbara sitting on her face while she ate her out. Elizabeth went down and parted Lara's legs, trailing her tongue along her fresh lap till she reached her center.

She opened her hot tempting mouth and sucked on her. Starting with the clit, she flipped it with her tongue up and down, sucking and licking her inner lips as she flipped. Lara continued to moan into Barbara's pussy, while she released hot breaths into her, making Barbara shiver and shake as she licked.

Elizabeth slid three fingers into Lara, rotating her fingers in her, as her clit throbbed.

One of Lara's hands managed to grab her hair, pulling her in for a mouthful as her clit thumped back and forward while her hips moved up and down. Gradually building to reach her climax, Lara could barely suck okay Barbara, who was frantically grinding her face, moaning to pleasure. Elizabeth slowed her swirling, guiding her back to Earth from her cloud Nine.

Feeling her hardened and open again, Elizabeth increased her quivering touch speed on Lara. Her mouth leaned toward her entrance, touching every hidden corner of her Bulbs, and she jerked her hips forward. She could feel the jerk of Lara's hips against her lips as her neck and back spines were arched, probably reading to release into her mouth.

Sucking on the bud of her clit, one last time, she held it in the warmth of her clit. As Lara reached her final destination, the subtle shock of it made her eyes open and her body jerk uncontrollably. Lara admired Elizabeth's long and thrilling tongue as it moved in and out of her, blurring her vision.

Elizabeth stood up, took a brown runner dick from her mini purse, and inserted it into her red and swollen center. It was big, but she managed to stuff it all in her. Once it was all in her, she released a hot liquid, while her legs continued to tremble.

Working runner dick in and out of her, with Barbara now sucking on her breast and biting her nipples, she wiggled her body like a wounded earthworm trying to Flee from salt. Elizabeth held her down and hastened her pace hard.

In a matter of minutes, Lara reached her climax, exploding and filling Elizabeth's mouth with the white liquid coming out of her entrance.

Satisfied with their big fin on the first day, they all decided to have their shower together in the bathroom, rubbing against each as they and kissing washed.

Elizabeth dresses up, picked up her bag, and left the two lovers, with the promise to come back for more, soon. Lara and Barbara were relieved to know that their little secret was safe from the public.

Once again, they were free to act as they wished, without fear or intimidation. They both managed to unpack their stuff, placing each in the right place and smacking backsides as they worked. At intervals, they would exchange kisses and light squeezes.

Their little secret was kept hidden till the end of their college days, with Elizabeth back for more.

The Princess

Once upon a time, in a kingdom far away, there lived a Muslim princess named Aisha. She was the youngest daughter of the Sultan and was known for her beauty, intelligence, and kindness. Aisha had always felt different from her sisters and had never been interested in the men that her father had chosen for her to marry.

Aisha was a free spirit, curious and adventurous, always seeking new knowledge and experiences. She loved to read and explore the world around her, even if it meant breaking the rules. But she kept her rebellious side hidden from her family, knowing that they expected her to behave like a proper princess.

One day, Aisha started attending a new school where she met a young and beautiful teacher named Fatima. From the moment they met, Aisha knew that she was in love with Fatima. They would spend hours talking and laughing together, and Aisha felt happier than she ever had before.

Fatima was unlike anyone Aisha had ever met. She was confident, intelligent, and independent, and she challenged Aisha's beliefs and values in the best possible way. Aisha was fascinated by her, drawn to her strength and beauty, and she couldn't help but feel a deep connection to her.

As their relationship grew stronger, Aisha knew that she had to tell her family about her feelings for Fatima. But she also knew that her family would never accept her being a lesbian, especially since they were devout Muslims.

Aisha agonized over how to tell them, going back and forth between wanting to be honest and wanting to keep her secret safe. She loved her family dearly, and the thought of losing them terrified her. But she also knew that she couldn't keep this part of herself hidden forever.

One night, as she lay in bed, Aisha made the decision to come out to her family. She knew it would be risky, but she couldn't bear to live a lie any longer. She gathered her courage and went to her father's chambers, knowing that this conversation would change her life forever.

When she arrived, she found her father sitting at his desk, reading a letter. He looked up as she entered, his face stern and unyielding.

"Aisha, what brings you here at this hour?" he asked, his voice cold.

"Father, I have something to tell you," Aisha said, her heart pounding in her chest.

Her father put down the letter and leaned back in his chair, his expression growing even more serious.

"What is it, daughter?" he asked.

Aisha took a deep breath and forced herself to look him in the eyes.

"Father, I am in love with someone," she said. "And that someone is a woman."

There was a moment of silence as her father processed her words. Aisha could see the anger and disbelief in his eyes, and she braced herself for his reaction.

"You cannot be serious," he finally said, his voice low and dangerous. "You, a princess of this kingdom, cannot be involved in such unnatural behavior. It is against the laws of Allah and the traditions of our people."

Aisha felt her stomach drop as she realized the gravity of the situation. Her father was not going to accept her for who she was, and she was going to have to face the consequences.

"Father, I cannot help who I love," she said, trying to reason with him. "I know it's not what you expected, but please try to understand."

But her father was not interested in understanding. He stood up from his chair and paced around the room, his fists clenched.

"You have brought shame upon our family," he said. "I

As Aisha stepped out of the carriage and into the bustling courtyard of her new school, she was immediately struck by the vibrant energy of the students around her. She had always been a curious and eager learner, and she couldn't wait to immerse herself in the knowledge that awaited her here.

But as she made her way to her classroom, she couldn't help but feel a sense of unease. She knew that her family would never approve of her attending a school that wasn't run by their trusted religious leaders. But Aisha was determined to follow her own path, even if it meant going against her family's wishes.

As she entered her classroom, Aisha felt a sudden flutter in her chest as her eyes fell upon the teacher at the front of the room. Fatima was unlike anyone Aisha had ever met before. Her warm smile and gentle manner immediately put Aisha at ease, and she felt a strange pull towards her.

Throughout the course of the day, Aisha found herself stealing glances at Fatima whenever she could. She listened intently as Fatima spoke, her voice like honey in Aisha's ears. And when class was over, Aisha couldn't help but linger behind, hoping to catch another glimpse of the captivating teacher.

Days turned into weeks, and Aisha's infatuation with Fatima only grew stronger. They would talk for hours after class, discussing everything from their favorite books to their dreams for the future. Aisha felt a deep connection with Fatima, one that she couldn't quite explain.

But as much as Aisha loved spending time with Fatima, she couldn't ignore the nagging feeling of guilt that had settled in her chest. She knew that her family would never approve of her spending so much time with a woman, let alone one who wasn't a member of their faith.

Despite her fears, Aisha knew that she had to tell her family the truth. She couldn't keep this secret any longer, not when her heart was overflowing with love for Fatima. But she couldn't have anticipated the reaction that would follow.

Aisha woke up early, excited for her first day at her new school. She had always been a good student, but this was a chance to start fresh and make new friends. She got dressed in her favorite pink dress, braided her hair, and grabbed her backpack before heading out the door.

As she walked through the bustling streets of the city, Aisha couldn't help but feel a little nervous. She didn't know anyone at the school, and she was worried that she wouldn't fit in. But she reminded herself that this was a new beginning, a chance to be herself and explore new opportunities.

When she arrived at the school, Aisha was taken aback by its grandeur. It was a sprawling building with tall columns, manicured lawns, and a grand entrance. She felt intimidated, but also excited to be a part of such a prestigious institution.

As Aisha made her way to her first class, she noticed a group of girls huddled together, whispering and giggling. She tried to ignore them and focus on finding her classroom, but their stares and whispers made her feel self-conscious.

Just as she was about to give up, Aisha heard a soft voice behind her. "Excuse me, do you need help finding your class?" It was Fatima, the young teacher she had met earlier. Aisha felt a rush of relief and gratitude wash over her.

Fatima led Aisha to her classroom and introduced her to the other students. Aisha felt a wave of relief when she realized that they were all friendly and welcoming. They asked her about her hobbies, her family, and where she was from. Aisha felt like she had finally found a place where she belonged.

After class, Aisha and Fatima walked together to the school courtyard. They sat under a shady tree and talked about their interests, their dreams, and their favorite books. Aisha felt a connection with Fatima that she had never felt with anyone before.

As the days went on, Aisha and Fatima's bond grew stronger. They would share stories, exchange book recommendations, and sometimes even sneak out of school to explore the city together. Aisha knew that she was falling in love with Fatima, but she didn't know if Fatima felt the same way.

One day, while they were sitting under their favorite tree, Aisha gathered the courage to tell Fatima how she felt. "Fatima, there's something I need to tell you. I think I'm in love with you." Fatima looked at Aisha with a mix of surprise and tenderness. "Aisha, I had a feeling that you might feel that way. And I have to admit, I feel the same about you."

Aisha felt a surge of happiness and relief. She had never been so sure of anything in her life. She and Fatima held hands, their hearts beating in unison. They knew that their love was forbidden, but they were willing to risk everything to be together.

As the bell rang, signaling the end of the school day, Aisha and Fatima reluctantly let go of each other's hands. They knew that their love was dangerous, but they couldn't help the way they felt. They just hoped that they could keep their secret hidden, at least for a little while longer

Aisha woke up early the next morning, feeling a mix of excitement and nerves about her first day at the new school. She carefully chose her outfit, wanting to make a good impression, and styled her long dark hair into loose waves. As she looked at herself in the mirror, she wondered if anyone at the school would notice her, or if she would blend in with the crowd like she had always done before.

When Aisha arrived at the school, she was immediately struck by its beauty. It was a modern building with large windows and lush green gardens. Aisha had never seen anything like it before. She made her way to the front office, where she was greeted by a friendly woman who gave her a tour of the school.

As they walked around the campus, Aisha couldn't help but notice how many of the students were staring at her. She tried to ignore them, but it was hard not to feel self-conscious. Aisha had always been a shy person, and she was worried about making friends in her new school.

During her first class, Aisha sat quietly at her desk, listening to the teacher talk about algebra. She tried her best to pay attention, but her mind kept wandering to thoughts of Fatima. Aisha wondered if she would see her at school today, or if she would have to wait until her next Arabic class.

When the bell rang for lunch, Aisha gathered her things and made her way to the cafeteria. She looked around for a place to sit, but all the tables were full. Just as she was about to give up and eat alone, a voice called out to her.

"Hey, you're new here, right? Do you want to sit with us?"

Aisha turned around and saw a group of girls smiling at her. They seemed friendly enough, so she nodded and walked over to their table. As they introduced themselves, Aisha couldn't help but feel a sense of relief. Maybe this new school wouldn't be so bad after all.

As they ate their lunch, the girls chatted about their classes and the upcoming school dance. Aisha tried her best to join in, but she felt like an outsider. She had never been one for small talk, and she couldn't help but think about Fatima.

After lunch, Aisha had her Arabic class. She couldn't wait to see Fatima again. When she walked into the classroom, her heart skipped a beat. Fatima was there, standing at the front of the room, writing on the whiteboard.

Aisha took a seat in the back of the class, trying to play it cool. She didn't want anyone to know that she was so enamored with her teacher. As Fatima taught the class, Aisha tried to focus on the lesson, but her mind kept wandering to thoughts of what it would be like to be with Fatima.

After class, Aisha hung back, pretending to look at her notes. She waited until all the other students had left before making her way to the front of the room.

"Excuse me, Miss Fatima?" Aisha said, her heart pounding in her chest.

Fatima turned around and smiled at her. "Yes, Aisha? Is there something you need?"

Aisha felt her cheeks turn red. She had rehearsed what she was going to say a thousand times in her head, but now that the moment was here, she couldn't find the words.

"I, uh, just wanted to say that I really enjoyed your class today," Aisha said, feeling embarrassed.

Fatima chuckled. "Well, thank you, Aisha. I'm glad you found it interesting."

Aisha wanted to say more, but she didn't know how to continue the conversation. Instead, she grabbed her bag.

Aisha had always known that her family expected her to marry a man chosen for her by her father, the Sultan. It was a duty she was expected to fulfill, as a daughter of the royal family. However, when she met Fatima, her new teacher at the school she was attending, everything changed. Aisha felt a strong pull towards Fatima, and they quickly became close friends. They would spend hours talking about their interests, their dreams, and their lives.

Aisha soon began to realize that her feelings for Fatima went beyond mere friendship. She was drawn to her in a way that she couldn't explain, and it confused her. She had been brought up in a strict Islamic household and had been taught that homosexuality was a sin. Aisha knew that if she acted on her feelings, she would be going against everything she had been taught.

Aisha's confusion only grew as she spent more time with Fatima. She would catch herself staring at her, admiring her beauty and intelligence. She would feel her heart skip a beat whenever Fatima touched her, even if it was just a friendly pat on the back. Aisha was struggling to understand what was happening to her.

One day, while they were studying together, Fatima asked Aisha if everything was okay. Aisha hesitated for a moment before finally confessing that she was confused about her feelings for Fatima. She didn't know if what she was feeling was right or wrong, and she didn't know what to do about it.

Fatima listened patiently as Aisha poured out her heart. She told Aisha that love was a beautiful thing, and that it didn't matter who it was between, as long as it was true. Fatima also confided in Aisha that she had been in love with another woman in the past, and that it was perfectly normal to feel the way Aisha was feeling.

For Aisha, hearing this from someone she trusted and respected so much was a relief. She felt like she wasn't alone in her confusion anymore, and that maybe there was hope for her after all. Aisha knew that her family would never accept her if she told them the truth about her feelings for Fatima, but she also knew that she couldn't keep them bottled up inside forever.

In the weeks that followed, Aisha struggled to come to terms with her feelings. She spent countless hours reading books and researching online about homosexuality and Islam. She spoke to a few trusted friends about her situation, but no one could offer her any concrete advice. Aisha felt lost and alone, and she didn't know where to turn.

Despite her confusion, Aisha couldn't deny the way she felt about Fatima. She was drawn to her in a way that she had never experienced before, and she knew that she wanted to be with her more than anything else in the world. But she also knew that it would come at a great cost.

Aisha's inner turmoil only grew as she struggled with her feelings. She began to feel like she was living a double life, hiding her true self from the world around her. She didn't know how much longer she could keep up the facade.

Finally, one day, Aisha made a decision. She couldn't keep living in fear and confusion any longer. She knew that she had to tell her family the truth about her feelings for Fatima, no matter the cost. It was a decision that would change her life forever.

As the days went on, Aisha found herself more and more drawn to Fatima. They would spend hours after class talking about everything from their favorite books to their dreams for the future. Aisha found herself opening up to Fatima in a way that she never had with anyone else.

But despite her growing feelings, Aisha couldn't shake the feeling that what she was experiencing was wrong. She had been taught her whole life that homosexuality was a sin, and she didn't know how to reconcile her beliefs with her heart.

One day, while she was sitting alone in her room, Aisha couldn't help but think about Fatima. She felt a mix of happiness and guilt wash over her, and she didn't know what to do. She opened up her laptop and started to research homosexuality in Islam, hoping to find some answers.

As she delved deeper into the subject, Aisha found that the topic was much more complex than she had originally thought. There were many different interpretations of the Quran, and opinions on homosexuality varied greatly. Some scholars argued that homosexuality was a sin and condemned it outright, while others argued that it was not explicitly mentioned in the Quran and therefore open to interpretation.

Aisha felt even more confused after her research. She didn't know which interpretation to believe or how to reconcile her beliefs with her growing feelings for Fatima. She knew that if she acted on her feelings, she risked losing everything - her family, her friends, and her place in society.

Despite her confusion, Aisha couldn't help but feel drawn to Fatima. She looked forward to seeing her in class every day and felt a sense of longing whenever they were apart. Aisha knew that her feelings for Fatima were real, but she didn't know how to reconcile them with her beliefs.

As the weeks went on, Aisha tried to ignore her feelings for Fatima and focus on her studies. She tried to convince herself that what she was experiencing was just a passing phase, but deep down, she knew that it was much more than that.

One day, Aisha couldn't take it anymore. She knew that she had to talk to someone about her feelings, but she didn't know who to turn to. She decided to confide in her best friend, who she had known since childhood.

When Aisha told her friend about her feelings for Fatima, she was met with shock and disbelief. Her friend couldn't believe that Aisha was attracted to another woman, and she urged her to forget about her feelings and focus on finding a man to marry.

But Aisha couldn't forget about her feelings for Fatima. They consumed her thoughts and feelings, and she knew that she had to figure out a way to reconcile them with her beliefs. She continued to research homosexuality in Islam and tried to find a way to make sense of her feelings.

As the days turned into weeks, Aisha became more and more isolated. She couldn't confide in her family or friends, and she felt like she was living a double life. She was torn between her beliefs and her feelings, and she didn't know how to move forward.

But little did she know that her life was about to change forever.

Despite feeling confused and conflicted, Aisha couldn't help but feel drawn to Fatima. They continued to spend time together, and Aisha found herself opening up to her in ways she never had with anyone else. Fatima listened with a patient ear as Aisha shared her hopes and fears, her joys and sorrows.

One day, they went for a walk in the nearby park. As they strolled through the colorful autumn leaves, Fatima took Aisha's hand in hers.

Aisha felt a jolt of electricity run through her body at the touch, and she couldn't help but smile.

"Do you feel it too?" Fatima asked, looking into Aisha's eyes.

Aisha felt her cheeks flush with embarrassment. She didn't know how to answer. She was afraid that if she admitted her feelings, everything would change. But she couldn't deny the way she felt.

"I don't know what I feel," she said, finally.

Fatima smiled softly. "That's okay. We don't have to figure it all out right now. Just know that I care about you, Aisha. And I always will."

As they continued to walk, Aisha felt a sense of peace settle over her. She knew that she was lucky to have someone like Fatima in her life, someone who accepted her for who she was.

But at the same time, Aisha couldn't shake the feeling that something was wrong. She knew that her family would never approve of her feelings for Fatima, and she worried about what would happen if they found out

As the days passed, Aisha couldn't shake off the feelings she had for Fatima. She tried to suppress them, but they kept resurfacing every time they were together. Aisha was tormented by her conflicting emotions and didn't know what to do.

One day, after school, Fatima invited Aisha to her house for some tea. As they sat on the couch, sipping their tea, Fatima noticed that Aisha seemed troubled.

"What's wrong, Aisha? You look like you have something on your mind," Fatima said.

Aisha hesitated for a moment before finally speaking up. "Fatima, I have something to tell you, and I don't know how you'll react."

Fatima put down her tea and turned to face Aisha. "Whatever it is, you can tell me. I promise I won't judge you."

Aisha took a deep breath and looked into Fatima's eyes. "I think I'm in love with you, Fatima."

Fatima was taken aback by Aisha's confession. She had never thought of Aisha in that way before, but she was also surprised by the intensity of her own feelings for Aisha.

"Aisha, I don't know what to say. I care about you deeply, but we can't act on these feelings. It's not allowed in our culture or religion," Fatima said.

Aisha felt her heart sink as she heard Fatima's words. She had been hoping that Fatima would feel the same way, but she knew that her love for Fatima was doomed from the start.

"I understand, Fatima. I'm sorry. I shouldn't have said anything," Aisha said, feeling embarrassed and ashamed.

Fatima put her arm around Aisha and pulled her close. "Don't be sorry, Aisha. You can't help how you feel. We'll get through this together."

From that day on, Aisha and Fatima's relationship changed. They both knew that they couldn't act on their feelings, but they couldn't deny the bond that had formed between them. They continued to spend time together, but they were more cautious and reserved in their interactions.

Aisha felt torn between her love for Fatima and her loyalty to her family and religion. She didn't know how to reconcile the two, and she felt like she was living a double life.

As the weeks went by, Aisha's feelings for Fatima only grew stronger. She found herself thinking about her all the time and longing for her touch. Aisha knew that she had to tell her family about her feelings for Fatima, but she didn't know how they would react.

One day, Aisha decided that she couldn't keep her secret any longer. She had to come clean and tell her family the truth. She knew that it would be difficult, but she also knew that she couldn't live a lie any longer.

Aisha called a family meeting and sat nervously at the head of the table. She took a deep breath and began to speak. "I have something to tell you all, and it's not easy for me to say. I think I'm in love with someone, but it's not a man."

Aisha's family was stunned by her words. They had always seen her as the dutiful and obedient daughter, and they never expected her to stray from their traditions and beliefs.

Her father, the Sultan, was the first to react. "What are you saying, Aisha? This is not acceptable. Who is this person?"

Aisha hesitated for a moment before speaking again. "Her name is Fatima. She's a teacher at my school, and she's kind, smart, and

Fatima listened patiently as Aisha poured out her heart, understanding the struggle that Aisha was going through. She took Aisha's hands in hers, giving them a gentle squeeze. "Aisha, love is love, and it doesn't matter who it is between. You can't help who you fall in love with. You shouldn't feel ashamed or guilty for loving me. It's not a sin to love someone of the same gender."

Aisha looked into Fatima's eyes, seeing nothing but love and acceptance. She felt a weight lift from her shoulders as she realized that Fatima was right. Love was love, and it wasn't a sin to love someone of the same gender.

As the days went by, Aisha began to feel more comfortable with her feelings for Fatima. They spent more time together, and Aisha found herself falling deeper in love with her. But she knew that she couldn't keep her feelings a secret forever. She had to tell her family, even if it meant risking everything.

One evening, as Aisha sat in her room, she heard a knock on her door. It was her mother, and she looked worried. "Aisha, your father wants to speak with you in his study," her mother said.

Aisha's heart sank. She knew what this meant. Her father had found out about her feelings for Fatima, and he was going to confront her about it. She took a deep breath and followed her mother to her father's study.

As she entered the room, she saw her father sitting behind his desk, looking stern. "Aisha, we need to talk," he said.

Aisha sat down in front of him, feeling the weight of his disapproval. "Father, I know what this is about," she said.

Her father looked at her, his eyes cold. "Do you?" he asked. "Do you know what you have done to this family? Do you know how much shame you have brought upon us?"

Aisha felt her throat tighten, but she forced herself to remain calm. "Father, I can't help how I feel. I know that it may be difficult for you to understand, but I love Fatima."

Her father's face turned red with anger. "This is unacceptable, Aisha. We are Muslims, and our faith forbids this kind of behavior. You are disgracing this family, and I will not stand for it."

Aisha felt a tear roll down her cheek. She had hoped that her father would understand, but it was clear that he wouldn't. She stood up, ready to leave the room.

"Where do you think you're going?" her father asked.

"I'm leaving, father. I can't stay here if you're going to treat me like this."

Her father stood up, towering over her. "If you leave, you will be disowned. You will no longer be a part of this family, and you will have nothing."

Aisha looked at her father, feeling the weight of his words. But she knew that she couldn't deny her feelings for Fatima. She took a deep breath and stood up straight. "I have to be true to myself, father. I can't pretend to be something that I'm not."

Her father looked at her, his face filled with anger. "Then you leave me no choice. You are no longer my daughter."

Aisha felt her heart shatter as she left the room. She knew that her life would never be the same. But she also knew that she couldn't deny her love for Fatima, no matter what the cost.

Aisha's heart raced as she approached the door to Fatima's classroom. She paused for a moment, took a deep breath, and then knocked softly. The door opened, and Fatima smiled warmly at her.

"Aisha, what a nice surprise," Fatima said. "Please come in."

Aisha stepped into the classroom, and her eyes immediately scanned the room for any signs of disapproval from the other students. But to her relief, no one seemed to be paying attention to her.

As she took a seat next to Fatima, Aisha's mind raced with questions. She didn't know how to talk about her feelings, and she didn't know how Fatima would react if she did.

After a moment of awkward silence, Fatima turned to Aisha and said, "Is everything okay? You seem a little nervous."

Aisha bit her lip and then blurted out, "I think I might be in love with you."

Fatima's eyes widened in surprise, and she took a moment to compose herself before responding. "Aisha, I'm flattered, but I'm also your teacher. We can't have this kind of relationship."

Aisha's heart sank, and she felt tears welling up in her eyes. She had known it was a long shot, but she had hoped that Fatima might feel the same way.

"I understand," Aisha said, her voice barely above a whisper. "I'm sorry. I shouldn't have said anything."

Fatima placed a gentle hand on Aisha's shoulder. "Don't be sorry, Aisha. It's okay to have feelings. But we need to be careful. I'm your teacher, and we need to maintain a professional relationship."

Aisha nodded, and they spent the rest of the class in silence. As soon as the class ended, Aisha rushed out of the room, her heart heavy with disappointment.

For the next few days, Aisha avoided Fatima as much as possible. She was embarrassed and didn't know how to face her after confessing her feelings.

But Fatima didn't give up on her. She sought Aisha out and invited her to coffee, where they had a long and difficult conversation about their feelings.

Fatima explained that while she cared deeply for Aisha, she couldn't act on those feelings because of the power dynamic between them. As her teacher, Fatima had a responsibility to maintain a professional relationship with Aisha, and any romantic involvement would be inappropriate.

Aisha understood, but it didn't make the pain any easier to bear. She had never felt this way before, and she didn't know how to deal with the intensity of her emotions.

Over the next few weeks, Aisha struggled to come to terms with her feelings for Fatima. She tried to bury them, to push them aside and focus on her studies, but they wouldn't go away.

One day, while walking home from school, Aisha ran into a group of girls who had always made fun of her for being different. They taunted her, calling her names and making crude jokes.

Aisha tried to ignore them and keep walking, but they followed her, shouting insults and threats. Aisha felt her anger building inside her, and she turned to face them.

"Stop it!" she shouted. "Leave me alone!"

The girls only laughed and continued to taunt her. Aisha felt a surge of rage, and before she knew it, she was punching and kicking them with all her might.

The girls were caught off guard, and Aisha managed to get away before they could retaliate. She ran home, her heart racing with adrenaline and fear.

When she got home, she collapsed on her bed, tears streaming down her face. She didn't know.

Aisha knew that she couldn't keep her feelings for Fatima a secret forever, and she decided that it was time to tell her family the truth. She hoped that they would understand and accept her for who she was, but she also feared their reaction.

One evening, Aisha gathered her family together in the living room. Her heart was pounding, and her palms were sweating as she tried to find the courage to speak. Finally, she took a deep breath and began to talk.

"Father, Mother, brothers, sisters," she said, her voice trembling. "I have something important to tell you. I have fallen in love with someone, but it's not a man."

There was a stunned silence in the room as Aisha's family looked at her in shock. Her father's face turned red with anger, and her mother looked like she was about to faint. Her brothers and sisters looked at her with a mixture of disbelief and disgust.

"What are you talking about, Aisha?" her father thundered. "How dare you bring such shame upon our family! Who is this person that you have dishonored us with?"

Aisha took a deep breath and looked directly at her father. "Her name is Fatima, and I love her," she said quietly but firmly.

Her father's face turned even redder with rage. "Fatima? Who is this woman? And how dare you disgrace us by being a lesbian! This is against everything we stand for as Muslims! You are no daughter of mine!"

Aisha's heart sank as her worst fears were confirmed. Her family would never accept her for who she was. She felt a deep sense of shame and rejection wash over her as her father ordered her to leave the house and never come back.

Aisha knew that she had to leave immediately. She couldn't stay in her family's home knowing that she was no longer welcome there. She packed a bag with some clothes and other essentials and left the house, tears streaming down her face.

As she walked through the streets of the city, Aisha felt lost and alone. She had no idea where to go or what to do. She knew that she couldn't go back to her old life, but she also didn't know how to start a new one.

For the next few days, Aisha slept on park benches and begged for food from strangers. She felt like she had hit rock bottom, and she didn't know how to pick herself back up.

But then, she remembered Fatima. The thought of her gave Aisha hope and strength. She knew that she had to find Fatima and be with her, no matter what the cost.

Aisha set out to find Fatima, asking everyone she met if they had seen her. She searched for days, not knowing where to look, until finally, she stumbled upon a small café in a quiet corner of the city. And there was Fatima, sitting alone at a table, lost in thought.

When Fatima saw Aisha, she jumped up from her seat and ran to her, wrapping her arms around her. "Aisha, what happened? Why are you here?" she asked, concern etched on her face.

Aisha told Fatima everything that had happened with her family, and Fatima listened attentively, holding Aisha's hand and wiping away her tears.

"We'll find a way, Aisha," Fatima said, her voice full of determination. "We'll figure something out. We can't let them keep us apart."

And with those words, Aisha felt a glimmer of hope for the first time in days. She knew that she had found someone who loved her for who she was and who would stand by her no matter

As Aisha made her way through the crowded market, she noticed a group of men staring at her. She felt uneasy and quickened her pace, but they started following her. Aisha felt a knot form in her stomach as she realized that they were the same men who had attacked her and Fatima in the village.

She tried to lose them in the maze of alleys, but they were relentless. Suddenly, they surrounded her, blocking her path. Aisha felt a surge of panic and started backing away, but one of the men grabbed her arm.

"Come with us, you filthy lesbian," he spat.

Aisha struggled, but they were too strong for her. They dragged her through the market, pushing and shoving her as they went. Aisha's heart pounded in her chest as she wondered what they were going to do to her.

Finally, they reached a deserted alleyway, and Aisha saw their true intentions. They wanted to punish her for her "unnatural" behavior, and they had brought a whip with them.

Aisha knew that she had to think fast. She closed her eyes and whispered a prayer, drawing strength from her faith. She thought of Fatima and how much she loved her, and she knew that she couldn't give up.

With a sudden burst of energy, Aisha broke free from the men's grip and ran as fast as she could. She heard them shouting and chasing after her, but she didn't look back.

Aisha ran for what felt like hours, her feet pounding against the pavement. She was exhausted and terrified, but she didn't stop until she was sure that she had lost the men.

As she collapsed against a wall, gasping for breath, Aisha realized that she couldn't keep running forever. She knew that she needed to find a way to be with Fatima without risking her life.

Determined, Aisha made a decision. She would leave her country and seek asylum in a more liberal country. She knew that it would be a difficult journey, but she was willing to risk everything to be with the woman she loved.

And so, Aisha started to plan her escape. She gathered her few possessions and said goodbye to the only home she had ever known. With a heavy heart, she set out on a journey that would change her life forever.

As the days passed, Aisha began to feel more comfortable with her newfound identity. She started to explore the LGBT+ community online and found a sense of belonging in their stories and experiences. She also began to open up to her friends and family, who were surprised but ultimately supportive of her.

However, Aisha still struggled with the idea of coming out to her parents. She knew that it would be a difficult conversation, but she also knew that it was something she needed to do for her own happiness and authenticity.

One day, she mustered up the courage to sit down with her parents and tell them the truth about her feelings towards Fatima and her own identity. At first, her parents were shocked and didn't know how to react. They asked her many questions, some of which were uncomfortable and invasive. But Aisha answered them all honestly and patiently, trying to help her parents understand her better.

After many tears and long conversations, Aisha's parents finally came around to accepting her for who she is. They told her that they loved her no matter what and that they were proud of her for being brave enough to share her true self with them.

From that moment on, Aisha felt a weight lifted off her shoulders. She could finally be herself without fear of judgment or rejection. She continued to see Fatima, and their love for each other only grew stronger with each passing day.

In the end, Aisha learned that it's never too late to discover who you truly are and to love yourself for it. And although the journey may be difficult at times, it's always worth it to live a life that's true to yourself.

As Aisha continued to spend more time with Fatima, her feelings for her only grew stronger. She found herself thinking about her all the time and feeling a sense of longing whenever they were apart. Aisha tried to suppress her feelings, thinking that they were wrong and against her beliefs, but she couldn't help the way she felt.

One day, Fatima invited Aisha to go on a hike with her. Aisha eagerly agreed, happy for any opportunity to spend more time with her beloved teacher. As they walked through the lush green forest, they came across a beautiful waterfall. Fatima suggested that they take a break and enjoy the peaceful scenery.

As they sat by the waterfall, Aisha couldn't help but feel overwhelmed by her emotions. She turned to Fatima, tears streaming down her face, and confessed her love to her. Fatima was surprised and taken aback, but she listened patiently as Aisha poured out her heart.

Fatima gently explained to Aisha that their love was not wrong, and that love is a beautiful and natural feeling that can be experienced between anyone. She told Aisha that it was important to embrace her feelings and not be ashamed of who she was.

Over time, Aisha and Fatima's relationship continued to blossom. They went on more hikes and had long talks about their dreams and aspirations. Aisha felt more comfortable in her own skin, no longer burdened by the weight of her confusion and shame.

However, not everyone in Aisha's life was accepting of her relationship with Fatima. Her parents, who held traditional views on love and marriage, were furious when they found out about her feelings. They forbade her from seeing Fatima again, and even threatened to send her away to a boarding school.

Aisha felt torn between her love for Fatima and her loyalty to her family. She didn't know what to do, and the constant conflict left her feeling exhausted and sad. She confided in Fatima, who listened and comforted her, but she knew that ultimately, the decision was Aisha's to make.

As Aisha struggled with her conflicting emotions, she realized that she needed to follow her heart. She loved Fatima with all her heart and knew that she couldn't live without her. Despite the potential consequences, she decided to be true to herself and pursue her love for Fatima.

Aisha's parents were furious with her decision and disowned her, but Aisha knew that she had made the right choice. She and Fatima continued their relationship, facing obstacles and challenges along the way, but always supporting and loving each other through it all. Their love story was not conventional, but it was beautiful in its own way, a testament to the power of love and the courage to follow one's heart.

Aisha had been keeping her feelings for Fatima a secret for months, and it was starting to take a toll on her. She couldn't bear the thought of hiding her true self from the people she cared about, but she also knew that coming out could have serious consequences.

One day, Aisha mustered up the courage to confide in her best friend, Sarah. She sat her down and told her everything, from her first meeting with Fatima to the feelings that had developed over time. Sarah was shocked at first, but she quickly rallied behind her friend.

"You can't keep this a secret forever," Sarah said. "You deserve to be happy and true to yourself, and if Fatima feels the same way, then that's all that matters."

Encouraged by Sarah's support, Aisha decided to take the next step and come out to her parents. She sat them down one evening and took a deep breath.

"Mum, Dad, there's something I need to tell you," she said, her heart racing.

Her parents looked at her expectantly, and Aisha knew that there was no turning back now.

"I'm in love with someone," she said, her voice barely above a whisper. "And that someone is a woman."

There was a moment of stunned silence, and Aisha felt like the weight of the world was on her shoulders. But then her parents spoke, and their words took her by surprise.

"We love you no matter what," her mother said, tears welling up in her eyes. "You are our daughter, and we will always support you."

Aisha felt a wave of relief wash over her, and she hugged her parents tightly. She knew that coming out wouldn't be easy, but having her family's love and support made it all worth it.

As the weeks passed, Aisha came out to her friends, her teachers, and anyone who asked. She was no longer hiding who she was, and it felt liberating. And when she finally told Fatima how she felt, the other woman's eyes lit up with joy.

"I was hoping you would say that," Fatima said, taking Aisha's hand in hers. "I love you too, Aisha."

They shared a tender kiss, and Aisha felt like she was finally home. She had come out and found love, and nothing else mattered.

As the weeks passed, Aisha continued to attend the youth group meetings and became more involved in the community. She even volunteered to help plan the upcoming Ramadan celebration at the mosque.

One day, as Aisha was leaving the mosque after a youth group meeting, she saw Fatima walking towards her. Her heart began to race as she approached, unsure of what to say.

"Hey, Aisha," Fatima said with a smile.

"Hi, Fatima," Aisha replied, feeling her cheeks flush.

"I wanted to thank you for all your help with the Ramadan celebration. You've been a great asset to the planning committee," Fatima said.

Aisha beamed with pride at the compliment. "Thanks, it's been really fun working on it."

They chatted for a few more minutes before Fatima had to leave, and Aisha watched her walk away with a mix of emotions. She couldn't deny her attraction to Fatima, but she also knew that it was against her beliefs and the teachings of her community.

As the Ramadan celebration drew near, Aisha found herself more and more consumed by her feelings for Fatima. She couldn't focus on anything else and began to withdraw from her friends and family.

On the day of the celebration, Aisha arrived early to help set up. She saw Fatima across the room, smiling and greeting guests. Aisha's heart skipped a beat as she walked over to say hello.

"Hey, Aisha!" Fatima said with a warm smile. "Thanks again for all your help with this."

Aisha nodded, her throat tight with emotion. "Of course, it's been really great."

As the night wore on, Aisha couldn't help but steal glances at Fatima. She felt guilty for her feelings, but she couldn't help the way she felt. It wasn't until the end of the night, when everyone was cleaning up, that she finally worked up the courage to talk to Fatima about how she was feeling.

"Fatima, can I talk to you for a minute?" Aisha asked nervously.

"Sure, what's up?" Fatima replied, looking concerned.

Aisha took a deep breath before continuing. "I don't know how to say this, but...I have feelings for you. Romantic feelings."

Fatima's eyes widened in surprise. "Aisha, I don't know what to say. I'm flattered, but you know that kind of relationship isn't allowed in our community."

"I know, and I'm sorry. I just had to tell you how I feel," Aisha said, her eyes brimming with tears.

Fatima put a comforting hand on Aisha's shoulder. "It's okay, Aisha. I understand how confusing and difficult this must be for you. Just remember that Allah loves you and wants what's best for you."

Aisha nodded, feeling a mix of relief and sadness. She knew that her feelings for Fatima weren't going to disappear overnight, but she also knew that she had to trust in Allah and follow the teachings of her community. It was a difficult path, but she was determined to stay true to herself and her faith.

As the weeks passed, Aisha and Fatima became even closer. They spent more and more time together outside of school, going on walks in the park or having picnics by the lake. Aisha found herself falling deeper in love with Fatima every day.

But at the same time, Aisha was feeling increasingly anxious. She knew that her feelings for Fatima were wrong according to the teachings of her religion and culture. She was torn between her love for Fatima and her fear of what would happen if anyone found out.

One day, Aisha mustered up the courage to talk to Fatima about her feelings. To her surprise, Fatima listened with kindness and understanding. She told Aisha that love was a beautiful thing, and that she should follow her heart, even if it meant going against what others might think or believe.

With Fatima's support, Aisha decided to come out to her family and friends. She knew it wouldn't be easy, but she couldn't keep her feelings bottled up inside any longer.

To her relief, Aisha's family and friends were more accepting than she had expected. They were surprised at first, but they still loved and supported her, no matter who she loved.

Aisha and Fatima's relationship continued to grow stronger, and they eventually got married in a beautiful ceremony surrounded by their loved ones. They knew that their love was true and pure, and they were grateful to have found each other.

Looking back on her journey, Aisha realized that love had no boundaries or limitations. It was simply a matter of following your heart and being true to yourself. And with Fatima by her side, she knew that she would always be happy and loved.

As the weeks went by, Aisha and Fatima continued to grow closer. They spent time together outside of school, going to museums, trying new foods, and exploring the city. Aisha's feelings for Fatima only intensified, but she still didn't know what to do about them.

One day, Aisha was sitting alone in the school courtyard during lunchtime, lost in thought. She felt a tap on her shoulder and turned to see Fatima standing behind her, holding two sandwiches.

"I thought you might be hungry," Fatima said with a smile.

Aisha's heart fluttered at the sight of her. "Thank you," she replied, taking the sandwich from Fatima's outstretched hand.

They sat in silence for a moment, enjoying their lunch. Aisha was acutely aware of how close they were sitting, their arms touching.

"Can I ask you something?" Aisha finally spoke up, breaking the silence.

"Of course," Fatima replied, looking at Aisha with concern.

Aisha took a deep breath. "I don't know if this is something I should be feeling, but...I think I'm in love with you," she said, her voice barely above a whisper.

Fatima's eyes widened in surprise. She opened her mouth to speak, but no words came out.

"I'm sorry," Aisha said quickly, tears starting to form in her eyes. "I shouldn't have said anything. I'll leave you alone."

She stood up to leave, but Fatima caught her arm gently. "Wait," she said, her voice soft. "It's not that I don't feel something for you too, Aisha. But we have to be careful. We can't act on these feelings while you're still a student and I'm your teacher. It wouldn't be right."

Aisha nodded, tears streaming down her face. She knew that Fatima was right, but it didn't make the situation any easier to bear. They finished their lunch in silence, each lost in their own thoughts.

Aisha had finally found the strength to accept herself for who she truly was, and she was ready to move forward with her life. She continued to attend her therapy sessions, and with time, her relationships with her family and friends began to heal.

One day, while walking through the park, Aisha stumbled upon a group of people gathered around a woman playing music on her guitar. As she approached, the woman looked up and smiled at her. Aisha felt drawn to the woman's kind eyes and warm smile, and before she knew it, she was sitting next to her, listening to her play.

They struck up a conversation, and Aisha was amazed to find that the woman, named Sara, was also a Muslim and had faced many of the same struggles that Aisha had. They talked about their shared experiences, and Aisha felt an immediate connection with Sara.

As they continued to talk, Sara mentioned that she was part of a local LGBT support group. Aisha was hesitant at first, but Sara assured her that the group was a safe space for Muslim members and that she would be welcomed with open arms.

With a newfound sense of courage, Aisha decided to attend a meeting of the support group. She was nervous at first, but as she listened to the stories of the other members, she felt a sense of belonging that she had never experienced before.

Over time, Aisha became an active member of the group, volunteering her time and energy to help others who were struggling with their own identities. She found that by sharing her own story and offering support to others, she was able to find peace within herself.

Aisha knew that her journey was far from over, and that there would be many more challenges to come. But she also knew that she was not alone, and that with the love and support of her community, she could face anything that came her way.

As Aisha continued to explore her passion for art, she found herself becoming more and more drawn to the vibrant and diverse community that surrounded her. She made new friends who shared her interests and values, and she felt truly accepted and valued for the first time in her life.

One day, as she was walking through the city's bustling streets, Aisha came across a poster advertising a local art exhibition. The poster featured a striking image of a woman with a fierce gaze and flowing hair, and Aisha felt an immediate connection to the piece. Intrigued, she made her way to the gallery and was amazed by the beauty and diversity of the artwork on display.

As she wandered from painting to painting, Aisha couldn't help but notice how many of the artists had used their art to explore themes of identity, acceptance, and belonging. She saw images of queer couples holding hands, portraits of strong women of color, and powerful statements of resistance and solidarity. Aisha felt inspired by the courage and creativity of these artists, and she knew that she wanted to contribute to this movement in her own way.

With renewed determination, Aisha threw herself into her art, experimenting with new techniques and styles and pushing herself to express her most authentic self on the canvas. She found that the more she embraced her true identity and values, the more her art resonated with others and the more opportunities she had to share her work with the world.

Years later, Aisha looked back on her journey with gratitude and pride. She had faced many challenges along the way, but she had also discovered a strength and resilience that she never knew she had. Through her art, she had found a way to connect with others, to express her deepest emotions and beliefs, and to create beauty in a world that so often felt dark and divided. She knew that her journey was far from over, but she also knew that she was ready for whatever lay ahead, armed with the power of her own creativity and the knowledge that she was not alone.

As the days went by, Aisha became more and more comfortable with the idea of coming out to her family. She knew it would be difficult, but she also knew it was the right thing to do. She started to imagine what her life would be like if she could be open about her feelings for Fatima, and it filled her with hope and excitement.

One afternoon, as Aisha was sitting in her room thinking about all of this, she heard a knock at her door. It was her mother, and Aisha could tell from the look on her face that something was wrong.

"Sit down, Aisha," her mother said, motioning to the bed. Aisha did as she was told, her heart racing with anxiety.

"I've been talking to some of the other parents at your school," her mother began, "and they've been saying some things that have me worried."

Aisha's stomach dropped. She had no idea what her mother was talking about, but she had a sinking feeling in her gut that it was about her.

"What kind of things?" Aisha asked, her voice barely above a whisper.

"They've been saying that there's a student at your school who's been spreading some very... inappropriate ideas about love and relationships," her mother said, her eyes narrowed. "I need to know if you've been involved in any of this."

Aisha's mind was racing. Should she come out to her mother right then and there? It was clear that her mother was already suspicious, but she didn't know how her mother would react to the truth.

"I don't know what you're talking about, Mom," Aisha said, trying to keep her voice steady.

Her mother's expression softened slightly, but she still looked concerned. "Well, just be careful who you're spending your time with, okay? I don't want you getting caught up in anything that could hurt your future."

Aisha nodded, relief flooding through her. She knew that she couldn't keep her feelings for Fatima a secret forever, but for now, she was glad to have avoided a difficult conversation.

As her mother left the room, Aisha let out a deep breath. She knew that she would have to come out eventually, but for now, she was content to keep her secret safe. But deep down, she couldn't help but wonder how much longer she could go on living a lie.

As Aisha continued her journey of self-discovery, she found herself drawn to exploring more about her culture and religion. She began reading books and attending lectures on Islam and homosexuality, trying to find some answers to her questions.

One day, Aisha was browsing online when she stumbled upon a forum where people discussed their experiences as LGBTQ Muslims. She was hesitant to join at first, but she eventually mustered up the courage to create a profile and start engaging with others.

Through the forum, Aisha met people from all over the world who shared similar struggles and experiences. She was amazed at the amount of support and understanding she received from this online community, which she had never found in her own physical community.

Aisha's new friends on the forum encouraged her to attend an LGBTQ Muslim conference happening in a nearby city. Aisha was hesitant at first, but eventually decided to attend. At the conference, she met many other LGBTQ Muslims who were struggling with the same issues as her. They shared their stories, offered support and advice, and Aisha felt like she had found a community where she truly belonged.

As the conference came to a close, Aisha realized that she had come a long way since she first met Fatima. She had discovered a new side of herself that she had been too afraid to explore before, and she had found a community that accepted her for who she was.

Aisha returned home feeling more confident and secure in her identity than ever before. She knew that she still had a long journey ahead of her, but for the first time in a long time, she felt like she was moving in the right direction.

After the ceremony, Aisha and Fatima were surrounded by their loved ones, who congratulated them on their marriage. Aisha's parents were hesitant at first, but seeing their daughter so happy with Fatima, they eventually accepted their relationship and welcomed Fatima into the family.

The newlyweds spent their honeymoon traveling to different parts of the world, experiencing different cultures and cuisines. They even attended a pride parade in a foreign city, where they were both moved to tears by the love and support they received from the LGBTQ+ community.

As they settled into married life, Aisha and Fatima continued to face challenges, but they faced them together. They started a family, adopting two children who they loved as their own. They built a life filled with laughter, joy, and most importantly, love.

Looking back on her journey, Aisha knew that she was lucky to have found Fatima. She knew that their love was not only true but also strong enough to withstand any obstacle that came their way. She was grateful for the support of her family and friends, and most of all, she was grateful for the love of her life, Fatima.

As Aisha sat on the bench, she couldn't help but think about how much her life had changed in just a few short months. She had gone from feeling lost and confused to being surrounded by love and acceptance.

Suddenly, she felt a tap on her shoulder and turned to see Fatima standing there with a small smile on her face.

"Hey," Fatima said, taking a seat next to Aisha. "How are you feeling?"

Aisha looked at her, feeling a sense of warmth spread throughout her body. "I'm good," she said, a smile creeping onto her own lips. "Just thinking about everything that's happened."

Fatima nodded, her gaze fixed on Aisha's face. "It's been a wild ride, hasn't it?"

Aisha laughed, feeling a weight lift off her shoulders. "Yeah, you could say that."

They sat in comfortable silence for a few moments before Fatima spoke up again. "I wanted to talk to you about something."

Aisha looked at her, curious. "What is it?"

Fatima took a deep breath before speaking. "I know we've been friends for a while now, but I just wanted to be honest with you about my feelings. Aisha, I have feelings for you, and I don't know how else to say it."

Aisha's eyes widened in surprise, and she felt her heart racing in her chest. She had always suspected that Fatima might have feelings for her, but she had never been sure.

"I-I don't know what to say," Aisha stammered, feeling a mixture of emotions swirling inside her.

Fatima looked at her with a hopeful expression. "You don't have to say anything right now. I just wanted to be honest with you."

Aisha nodded, feeling a sense of relief wash over her. She had never been one to confront her feelings head-on, but now that she knew how Fatima felt, she couldn't ignore her own feelings any longer.

As the sun began to set, they sat together on the bench, lost in their own thoughts. Aisha knew that her life was about to change once again, but this time, she was ready for it. She was ready to explore her feelings for Fatima and see where they might lead.

As the days went by, Aisha and Fatima continued to grow closer. They spent every spare moment together, talking, laughing, and enjoying each other's company. Aisha's feelings for Fatima only continued to grow, and she found herself thinking about her constantly.

However, Aisha couldn't shake the feeling of guilt that nagged at the back of her mind. She had been taught all her life that love between two women was wrong, and she couldn't reconcile that belief with her feelings for Fatima.

One day, Aisha decided to talk to her mother about what was going on. She took a deep breath and sat down with her mother, explaining everything that had been going on at school and how she felt about Fatima. To her surprise, her mother listened calmly and sympathetically.

"I understand that this must be difficult for you, Aisha," her mother said gently. "But you have to remember that love comes in many forms, and it is not up to anyone else to dictate who you can or cannot love. If you feel a strong connection with Fatima, then you should explore that and see where it leads."

Aisha felt a weight lift off her shoulders as she listened to her mother's words. For the first time, she felt like it was okay to be who she was and to love who she loved.

With her mother's encouragement, Aisha continued to spend time with Fatima and explore her feelings. She found herself falling deeper and deeper in love with her, and she knew that she wanted to spend the rest of her life with her.

One day, after school, Aisha worked up the courage to confess her love to Fatima. She took a deep breath and told Fatima everything, pouring her heart out to her.

To Aisha's relief, Fatima listened intently and then took her hand, squeezing it gently. "Aisha, I had no idea that you felt this way," she said softly. "I care for you deeply, but I want to make sure that you are comfortable with this. We can take things slow and see where this goes, if that's what you want."

Aisha felt her heart swell with happiness as she realized that Fatima felt the same way about her. They embraced, and Aisha knew that she had found the person she wanted to spend the rest of her life with.

Together, they faced the challenges of being in a same-sex relationship in a society that often frowned upon it. But with each other's love and support, they knew that they could overcome anything.

Years later, as they stood together on their wedding day, Aisha looked into Fatima's eyes and knew that she had made the right choice. She had followed her heart and found her soulmate, and she knew that they would spend the rest of their lives together, no matter what challenges lay ahead

As the days passed, Aisha realized that she couldn't keep her feelings for Fatima hidden anymore. She knew that she had to tell her family and friends, but the thought of their reactions made her anxious.

One day, she sat her family down and took a deep breath. "I have something important to tell you," she began. "I'm in love with someone, but it's not a man. It's Fatima, my teacher."

Her family was shocked and didn't know how to react. Her mother started to cry, while her father was angry and refused to accept it. They couldn't understand how Aisha could be attracted to another woman.

Aisha's friends were more supportive, but she still faced discrimination and judgment from some of them. She was called names and excluded from social events.

Despite the backlash, Aisha stood firm in her identity and refused to hide who she was. She found comfort in a supportive group of friends and allies, and slowly but surely, the negative attitudes around her began to shift.

One day, Fatima took Aisha's hand and looked into her eyes. "I'm proud of you," she said. "You're brave and strong, and you deserve to love who you love."

Aisha smiled, feeling grateful for Fatima's unwavering support. She knew that coming out was a difficult journey, but she also knew that it was the right thing to do for herself and for others who may be struggling with their identities.

After the concert, Aisha and Fatima joined the rest of the school in the cafeteria for a celebratory dinner. As they ate, Aisha couldn't help but notice the way Fatima's eyes sparkled when she talked about music. She found herself feeling grateful for their shared love of music, and for the opportunity to have gotten to know Fatima.

As the night came to a close, Aisha walked Fatima to her car. They hugged and said goodnight, but Aisha lingered for a moment, looking up at Fatima's face. Without thinking, she leaned in and kissed her. Fatima seemed surprised at first, but then she kissed Aisha back.

"I've been wanting to do that for a long time," Aisha said, smiling.

"Me too," Fatima replied, taking Aisha's hand.

From that moment on, Aisha and Fatima were inseparable. They spent their free time exploring the city, trying new foods, and attending concerts and other cultural events. Aisha felt like she had finally found someone who truly understood her, and who loved her for who she was.

However, their relationship was not without its challenges. Aisha's family did not approve of her relationship with Fatima, and they frequently argued about it. Aisha felt torn between her love for Fatima and her loyalty to her family, and it caused her a great deal of emotional pain.

Despite the challenges, Aisha and Fatima continued to love each other fiercely. They supported each other through difficult times, celebrated each other's successes, and remained devoted to each other no matter what.

In the end, Aisha knew that her love for Fatima was worth fighting for, and she was willing to do whatever it took to make their relationship work. As they stood on a rooftop terrace, overlooking the city they both loved, Aisha took Fatima's hand and said, "I don't know what the future holds, but I do know that I love you, and I want to spend the rest of my life with you."

Fatima's eyes filled with tears as she replied, "I love you too, Aisha. And I promise to always be here for you, no matter what."

With those words, Aisha felt her heart swell with love and gratitude. She knew that life would continue to present challenges, but as long as she had Fatima by her side, she could face anything. Together, they embraced the future, ready to conquer whatever lay ahead.

As the days went by, Aisha found herself more and more drawn to Fatima. They continued to spend time together outside of school, going to movies and restaurants, and Aisha found that she couldn't stop thinking about her.

One day, Aisha decided to take a chance and confess her feelings to Fatima. She was nervous and scared, but she knew that she had to be honest with herself and with Fatima.

To her surprise, Fatima listened to Aisha's confession with an open heart and an understanding smile. She gently explained to Aisha that she was flattered, but that she didn't feel the same way.

Aisha was devastated, but she tried her best to be understanding. She knew that she couldn't force someone to love her back, and she respected Fatima's honesty.

Over time, Aisha and Fatima's relationship shifted back to being just teacher and student. It wasn't always easy, and there were moments when Aisha couldn't help but feel a twinge of sadness when she thought about what could have been.

But she also knew that she had grown so much through her experiences with Fatima. She had learned to be true to herself, even when it was scary, and she had discovered the power of vulnerability and honesty.

And who knows what the future might hold? Aisha had learned that love comes in all shapes and forms, and that sometimes the most unexpected connections can be the ones that change your life the most.

After a few days, Aisha's father finally arrived in town. Aisha was nervous about how he would react to her coming out as a lesbian, but she knew it was important to be honest with him. When they sat down to talk, Aisha explained her feelings for Fatima and her confusion about how to reconcile her beliefs with her heart.

At first, her father was stunned and didn't know what to say. But then he looked at Aisha with a gentle expression and told her that he loved her no matter what. He explained that he may not fully understand her feelings, but that he would always support her and be there for her.

Aisha felt a weight lifted off her shoulders and a sense of relief wash over her. She was grateful for her father's acceptance and love, and it gave her the courage to continue being true to herself.

As the days passed, Aisha and Fatima grew closer and closer. They went on walks together, talked about their hopes and dreams, and supported each other through the ups and downs of life.

One day, Fatima surprised Aisha with a beautiful picnic in the park. As they sat on the blanket, enjoying the sunshine and each other's company, Fatima took Aisha's hand and looked deeply into her eyes. "Aisha, I know we've only known each other for a short time, but I can't imagine my life without you. Will you be my girlfriend?"

Aisha's heart skipped a beat as tears welled up in her eyes. She looked at Fatima, feeling overwhelmed with emotion, and whispered, "Yes, I will."

From that moment on, Aisha and Fatima's relationship blossomed into a beautiful love story. They faced challenges along the way, but with the support of their friends and family, they were able to overcome them and build a life full of love and happiness.

Years later, as they sat together on the porch of their cozy home, Aisha looked at Fatima and smiled. "I'm so glad I had the courage to be true to myself and follow my heart," she said.

Fatima took her hand and squeezed it gently. "Me too, my love. Me too."

As time passed, Aisha and Fatima's relationship continued to grow stronger. They became each other's confidante and best friend. Aisha's parents noticed the positive changes in her and were happy that she was finally coming out of her shell. They were unaware of her true feelings for Fatima.

One day, Aisha overheard a group of students gossiping about her and Fatima's close relationship. They were using words like "lesbian" and "unnatural" to describe them. Aisha was hurt and confused by their words. She didn't know what to do or how to react.

Aisha started to distance herself from Fatima, avoiding her at all costs. Fatima noticed the change in Aisha's behavior and tried to talk to her about it, but Aisha refused to listen. She was afraid of what others would think of her if she continued her relationship with Fatima.

Fatima was heartbroken by Aisha's actions, but she didn't give up on her. She wrote Aisha a letter expressing her feelings and telling her that she would always be there for her, no matter what. Aisha read the letter and was moved by Fatima's words. She realized that she had been letting other people's opinions control her own feelings.

Aisha decided to confront the students who had been gossiping about her and Fatima. She stood up for herself and her relationship, telling them that love is love, no matter who it is between. The students were taken aback by Aisha's confidence and bravery.

After that day, Aisha and Fatima's relationship continued to flourish. They didn't care about what other people thought of them because they knew that their love was true and genuine. Aisha finally felt comfortable in her own skin and was grateful for the love and support of Fatima.

After the ceremony, Aisha and Fatima decided to take a walk around the city. They held hands and talked about their future plans. Aisha felt happy and content with Fatima by her side.

As they were walking, they came across a group of people protesting against same-sex relationships. Aisha felt her heart drop, and she felt scared. Fatima held her hand tightly and pulled her away from the protestors, telling her not to pay attention to them.

Aisha couldn't believe that there were still people who were so against love between two people, no matter their gender. It made her sad, but it also made her more determined to stand up for what she believed in.

As they continued their walk, they stumbled upon a park. They sat down on a bench and watched children play. Aisha couldn't help but think about how much she wanted to have a family with Fatima. She knew it wouldn't be easy, but she was willing to fight for it.

As the sun began to set, they made their way back home. Aisha felt grateful for this day and for the love that she and Fatima shared. She knew that it wasn't going to be easy, but she was willing to face any obstacle for the sake of their love.

When they reached home, they cuddled up on the couch and watched a movie. Aisha felt safe and loved in Fatima's arms. She knew that no matter what challenges they faced in the future, they would face them together.

Aisha sat in her room, staring at the blank canvas in front of her. She had finally come to terms with her feelings for Fatima, and now she had a new sense of clarity and purpose. She picked up her paintbrush and began to create.

As she painted, she thought about all the ups and downs she had experienced in her journey of self-discovery. She had faced so many obstacles, but she had never given up. She had learned to love and accept herself, and that was the most important thing.

Suddenly, there was a knock at the door. It was Fatima. Aisha's heart skipped a beat as she let her in.

"I just wanted to check on you," Fatima said, looking at the painting in progress.

Aisha felt a rush of nervous energy as she showed Fatima her work. But as she watched Fatima's eyes light up with admiration, all her anxiety melted away.

"It's beautiful," Fatima said, placing a hand on Aisha's shoulder. "You're truly talented."

Aisha beamed with pride and happiness, feeling a sense of validation she had never experienced before. She realized that her journey of self-discovery had led her to a new beginning, and she was excited to see what the future held.

As the days passed, Aisha and Fatima grew closer than ever before. They shared their dreams and aspirations, and supported each other in every way possible. Aisha finally felt like she belonged somewhere, and that she had found her place in the world.

One day, Fatima took Aisha to a local gallery to show her work. Aisha was blown away by the art on display, and felt a sense of inspiration and motivation she had never experienced before.

"I want to do this," she said, turning to Fatima. "I want to be an artist."

Fatima smiled, a look of pride and affection in her eyes. "I know you can do anything you set your mind to," she said.

From that moment on, Aisha dedicated herself to her art, honing her skills and refining her techniques. She entered contests and exhibitions, and soon her work was being recognized and celebrated by art enthusiasts and collectors alike.

Aisha had finally found her true calling, and she knew that none of it would have been possible without the love and support of Fatima.

As the years passed, Aisha and Fatima continued to inspire and uplift each other. They remained inseparable, sharing a bond that transcended time and distance.

And as Aisha looked back on her journey of self-discovery, she realized that it had all been worth it. She had overcome her fears and doubts, and had emerged stronger and more confident than ever before.

She had found love, acceptance, and a sense of purpose, and she knew that she would continue to thrive and grow for the rest of her life.

As Aisha continued to study and work towards her goals, she found herself becoming more comfortable in her own skin. She no longer felt the need to hide her true self, and her relationships with her family and friends became stronger as a result.

One day, while browsing through social media, Aisha came across a post from Fatima. It was a photo of her and her partner, smiling and happy together. Aisha felt a pang of jealousy, but also a sense of relief. She realized that Fatima had moved on and was happy in her own life, and that it was time for Aisha to do the same.

She continued to focus on her studies and her career, but also made an effort to meet new people and explore her own interests. She started going to local LGBT events and making connections with others in the community. She even met someone special, a kind and supportive person who made her feel loved and accepted for who she truly was.

As she looked back on her journey, Aisha realized that coming out was not easy, but it was worth it. It had allowed her to be true to herself, to find love and acceptance, and to live a life that was authentic and fulfilling. She knew that there would be challenges along the way, but she was ready to face them with courage and determination.

As the days passed, Aisha and Fatima's relationship grew stronger. They shared everything with each other and talked about their dreams, hopes, and fears. Aisha felt safe and comfortable with Fatima, and she knew that Fatima felt the same way.

One day, as they sat in a park, Fatima looked at Aisha with a serious expression. "Aisha, I need to talk to you about something," she said.

Aisha's heart skipped a beat. She wondered what Fatima was going to say. "What is it?" she asked, trying to keep her voice steady.

Fatima took a deep breath. "I know that you've been struggling with your feelings for me," she said. "And I want you to know that I feel the same way. I love you, Aisha."

Aisha's eyes widened in surprise. She had never expected Fatima to say those words. But as she looked into Fatima's eyes, she knew that they were true. She loved Fatima, and she wanted to be with her.

Tears rolled down Aisha's cheeks as she leaned in to kiss Fatima. It was a gentle, sweet kiss that spoke volumes about the love they shared. They sat there for a while, holding each other and whispering words of love.

From that day on, Aisha and Fatima were inseparable. They faced many challenges and obstacles, but their love for each other gave them the strength to overcome them all. They knew that they were meant to be together, and they were willing to fight for their love no matter what.

As they walked hand in hand, Aisha felt a sense of peace and contentment that she had never felt before. She knew that she had found her soulmate in Fatima, and she was grateful for every moment they spent together.

As the days passed, Aisha and Fatima grew closer and closer. They shared more intimate moments and even talked about their future together. Aisha had never felt so happy and loved, but at the same time, she couldn't shake the feeling of guilt that gnawed at her.

One day, Aisha's mother visited her at school and noticed how close Aisha and Fatima had become. She questioned Aisha about their relationship, and Aisha found herself struggling to come up with a satisfactory answer.

"I don't know, Mom," she finally admitted. "I just know that I love her and she loves me, and I can't imagine my life without her."

Aisha's mother was shocked and didn't know how to react. She had always believed that love was between a man and a woman, and the idea of her daughter being in a same-sex relationship was foreign to her.

Aisha tried to explain her feelings to her mother, but it only made things worse. Her mother became increasingly upset and demanded that she end things with Fatima.

"I can't do that, Mom," Aisha said firmly. "I love her."

Her mother sighed and looked at her with a pained expression. "I just don't understand, Aisha. Why can't you be like everyone else?"

Aisha felt a pang of hurt at her mother's words, but she knew that she couldn't change who she was. She loved Fatima, and that was all that mattered.

As the days went on, Aisha's mother continued to pressure her to end things with Fatima, but Aisha remained steadfast in her love for her girlfriend. She knew that it wouldn't be easy, but she was willing to fight for their relationship.

Finally, after much discussion and tears, Aisha's mother began to accept their relationship. It wasn't easy, but she loved her daughter and wanted her to be happy.

Aisha and Fatima continued to be inseparable, and they knew that they had each other's love and support no matter what. They dreamed of a future together, one where they could be free to love each other without fear or judgment.

In the end, Aisha realized that love was love, no matter who it was between. She had found her soulmate in Fatima, and nothing could change that.

As the weeks went by, Aisha and Fatima continued to grow closer. They would spend their free time together, exploring the city and trying new foods. Aisha had never felt so alive and happy, and she knew it was because of Fatima.

However, there were moments when Aisha felt a twinge of sadness. She knew that her family would never accept her love for Fatima, and she didn't know how to reconcile her heart with her culture and religion. She confided in Fatima about her fears, and Fatima listened with empathy and understanding.

One day, as they were walking in the park, Aisha saw a group of girls from her old school. Her heart started pounding with fear as memories of their bullying flooded back to her. But to her surprise, Fatima stepped forward and stood by her side, her hand holding Aisha's tightly. The girls sneered and made rude comments, but Fatima remained calm and composed, never once letting go of Aisha's hand.

As they walked away, Aisha felt a surge of gratitude and love for Fatima. She knew that their love would face many challenges, but she was willing to face them all as long as she had Fatima by her side. They continued walking, their hands still intertwined, and Aisha felt as though nothing in the world could tear them apart.

Aisha had made the decision to move on from her past and start living her life for herself. She enrolled in university and began studying for a degree in psychology. Her experiences had given her a deep understanding of the human psyche, and she was determined to use her knowledge to help others.

As she began her studies, Aisha also started to explore her own interests and passions. She joined a club for hiking enthusiasts and discovered a love for the great outdoors. She also started to attend local poetry readings and discovered a talent for writing.

One day, while she was out hiking, she met a woman named Hira. They struck up a conversation and quickly realized they had a lot in common. Hira was a writer and photographer, and the two of them bonded over their shared love of creative expression.

As they got to know each other better, Aisha began to develop feelings for Hira. She was hesitant at first, still unsure about her own sexuality and afraid of getting hurt again. But Hira was patient and understanding, and she encouraged Aisha to open up and explore her feelings.

Eventually, Aisha came to the realization that she was in love with Hira. She was scared to tell her, afraid of what might happen, but she knew that she couldn't keep her feelings hidden forever.

One day, while they were sitting on a hill overlooking the city, Aisha took a deep breath and confessed her feelings to Hira. To her surprise, Hira smiled and took her hand.

"I know," she said. "And I feel the same way."

Aisha felt a weight lifted off her shoulders. For the first time in a long time, she felt truly happy and content. She knew that there would be challenges ahead, but with Hira by her side, she was ready to face them head-on.

Together, they continued to explore their interests and passions. Aisha's studies in psychology gave her a new perspective on life, and she found joy in helping others. Hira's creativity and artistic vision inspired Aisha, and they often collaborated on projects together.

As they walked hand-in-hand through the city streets, Aisha couldn't help but think about how far she had come. She had faced her fears, overcome her doubts, and found love in the most unexpected place. She knew that there would be ups and downs, but she was ready for whatever came her way. For the first time in a long time, she felt truly alive.

As Aisha and Fatima started their new journey together, they faced many challenges. One of the biggest challenges was coming out to their families and friends. Aisha's parents were shocked and initially disapproving of her relationship with Fatima, but they eventually came to accept and support their daughter's love. Fatima's family, however, was not as accepting, and she struggled with their disapproval.

Despite these challenges, Aisha and Fatima were happy and in love. They found strength in each other and continued to build a life together. They traveled the world, explored new cultures, and made many new friends.

As they settled into their new life together, they also became active members of their local LGBTQ+ community. They volunteered at a local LGBTQ+ center and marched in pride parades together. They found purpose in advocating for equality and supporting others who were going through similar struggles.

Over time, Aisha and Fatima's relationship deepened even further. They talked about getting married and starting a family. They discussed their hopes and dreams for the future and supported each other through both the highs and the lows.

One day, as they were walking through the park, Fatima got down on one knee and proposed to Aisha. Aisha was overjoyed and said yes without hesitation. They held a beautiful wedding ceremony surrounded by their loved ones and started their journey as a married couple.

As they looked back on their journey, Aisha and Fatima were grateful for the love and support they had received along the way. They knew that their journey was not easy, but they were proud of the life they had built together. They continued to advocate for equality and support others in the LGBTQ+ community, hoping to make the journey easier for others in the future.

Their love story was a testament to the power of love and the strength of the human spirit. They had overcome countless obstacles and emerged stronger together. Aisha and Fatima knew that their journey was far from over, but they were excited to see where life would take them next.

Aisha had come a long way since her arrival at the new school. She had faced challenges, overcome her fears, and discovered her true self. She had also found love in the most unexpected place.

As the school year came to an end, Aisha and Fatima had to say goodbye to each other. Fatima was moving to a different city to pursue her dream job, and Aisha was staying behind to finish her studies. They both knew that their relationship would not be easy, but they were determined to make it work.

Aisha had learned to accept herself for who she was, and she was no longer afraid to show it to the world. She had found love, and she was ready to fight for it.

The summer break gave Aisha the time she needed to reflect on the past year. She thought about all the things she had learned, the people she had met, and the experiences she had had. She realized that she had grown a lot, and that she was excited to see what the future held for her.

As the new school year began, Aisha felt a sense of excitement and anticipation. She was looking forward to the new challenges and opportunities that lay ahead. She was also looking forward to seeing Fatima again, who had promised to visit her whenever she could.

Aisha knew that she still had a lot to learn, but she was no longer afraid of the unknown. She had found the courage to follow her heart, and she was ready to face whatever came her way.

In the end, Aisha realized that life was full of surprises, and that the journey was just as important as the destination. She had learned to embrace her true self, to love without fear, and to never give up on her dreams. She knew that the road ahead would not be easy, but she was ready to take it on with courage and determination.

As Aisha and Fatima continued to explore the world together, they discovered new places and had new experiences. They went on hikes in the mountains, visited art galleries, and tried new restaurants. Each experience brought them closer together, and they found that they could talk about anything and everything with each other.

One day, as they were sitting on a bench overlooking a beautiful lake, Fatima turned to Aisha and said, "I have something to tell you." Aisha's heart started beating faster as she waited for Fatima to continue.

"I love you, Aisha," Fatima said softly. "I know we've been best friends for a long time, but I can't deny how I feel about you anymore. I want to be with you."

Aisha was taken aback. She had suspected that Fatima might have feelings for her, but she had never expected her to confess her love so boldly. Aisha took a deep breath before responding.

"Fatima, I love you too," she said. "But I'm scared. I don't know what our families will think, or how society will treat us. I don't want to lose you, but I'm afraid of the consequences."

Fatima took Aisha's hand and gave it a reassuring squeeze. "I know it won't be easy," she said. "But we can face whatever comes together. I love you more than anything, and I want to be with you."

Aisha felt a weight lift off her shoulders as she realized that Fatima was right. They could face the challenges ahead as long as they had each other. They hugged each other tightly, knowing that they were about to embark on a new journey together.

As Aisha entered the car, she was met with the familiar scent of leather and the warmth of the sun that had been shining down on the car. She took a deep breath and tried to calm her nerves, but her mind was racing with thoughts and emotions.

As they drove down the highway, Aisha couldn't help but think about all that had happened in the past few days. She felt grateful for her friends and family who had supported her through it all, but she also felt a sense of sadness and loss.

She wondered what her life would be like now that she had come out and embraced her true self. Would she be accepted by her community and society? Would she find love and companionship?

Aisha's thoughts were interrupted by her mother's voice. "Aisha, are you okay? You seem lost in thought."

Aisha looked up and forced a smile. "Yes, I'm okay. Just thinking about things."

Her mother placed a hand on her shoulder. "You know we love you no matter what, right?"

Aisha nodded, feeling a sense of warmth and comfort from her mother's words.

As they continued driving, Aisha looked out the window and saw the city skyline in the distance. She felt a sense of excitement and possibility wash over her.

Maybe this was the beginning of a new chapter in her life. A chapter filled with self-discovery, love, and acceptance.

Aisha was ecstatic as she received the letter of acceptance to the prestigious university. She couldn't believe that she had been chosen for the scholarship program. She hugged Fatima tightly, thanking her for the support and encouragement throughout the application process.

As she started her university journey, Aisha found herself thriving academically and socially. She had made new friends and was deeply involved in various student organizations. She was also delighted to discover that the university had an LGBTQ+ club, which provided a safe space for students like her to come together and discuss their experiences.

Aisha became an active member of the club, attending meetings and events regularly. She even became a volunteer at the annual Pride Parade and Festival, which was a huge success. She was proud to be part of the community and wanted to make a positive impact on the lives of others.

However, Aisha's happiness was short-lived as she faced discrimination and homophobia from some of her classmates and professors. She was devastated when a professor refused to acknowledge her preferred name and pronouns, insisting on using her birth name and referring to her as "she" instead of "they."

Aisha was disheartened by the lack of understanding and acceptance from some people around her, but she refused to let it bring her down. She continued to speak up and fight for her rights, determined to make a difference. She attended protests and rallies, advocating for LGBTQ+ rights and inclusion.

One day, Aisha received a call from her mother, who tearfully apologized for her past behavior and expressed her unconditional love and support for Aisha. Her mother had realized that her daughter's happiness was more important than societal norms and expectations. Aisha was overjoyed to hear her mother's words and knew that she had come a long way in her journey towards self-acceptance and understanding.

As Aisha graduated from university with flying colors, she looked back at her journey and felt grateful for all the experiences that had made her who she was. She was proud of herself for overcoming the obstacles and standing up for what she believed in. As she walked across the stage to receive her diploma, she knew that she was ready to face the world and make a difference in the lives of others.

As they approached the shore, Aisha's heart began to race. She knew that this was the moment she had been waiting for, the moment when she would finally be reunited with her love. The boat docked, and Aisha stepped out onto the sandy beach.

Suddenly, she saw her, standing at the water's edge, looking out over the sea. Fatima turned around, and their eyes met. Aisha could feel her heart pounding in her chest as she walked towards her.

When she was only a few feet away, Fatima reached out her hand and took Aisha's in hers. They stood there for a moment, looking at each other, and then they both started to laugh. It was a beautiful, joyful sound, and Aisha felt a sense of peace wash over her.

Together, they walked along the beach, hand in hand, the waves lapping at their feet. They talked about everything and nothing, and Aisha felt happier than she ever had before.

As the sun began to set, they sat down on the sand, still holding hands. Aisha leaned her head on Fatima's shoulder, and they watched the sky turn from blue to pink to orange. It was the most beautiful sunset Aisha had ever seen, and she knew that she would never forget this moment.

As the stars came out and the moon rose in the sky, they continued to sit there, lost in each other's company. Aisha knew that this was where she belonged, with the woman she loved, in this beautiful, peaceful place.

Finally, as the night wore on, they stood up and started to walk back towards the boat. Aisha felt a sense of sadness wash over her as she realized that this perfect day was coming to an end. But she also felt a sense of hope, knowing that she and Fatima would always have this moment, this memory to hold onto.

As they climbed back onto the boat and started to sail away from the island, Aisha looked back at the shore, knowing that she would return one day, to this place where she had found true love.

Aisha and Fatima had been together for almost three years now, and their love for each other had only grown stronger. They had talked about spending the rest of their lives together, but Aisha was still waiting for the right moment to propose.

One evening, as they were sitting on the couch cuddling, Aisha mustered up the courage to bring up the topic of marriage.

"Fatima, I love you more than anything in this world, and I want to spend the rest of my life with you," Aisha said, her heart racing with nervousness.

Fatima's eyes lit up with joy, and she took Aisha's hands in hers. "Aisha, I love you too, and I can't imagine my life without you," she replied.

Aisha took a deep breath before continuing. "Fatima, will you marry me?" she asked, holding out a small velvet box with a diamond ring inside.

Fatima gasped in surprise and tears of happiness filled her eyes. "Yes, Aisha! I will marry you," she exclaimed, pulling Aisha into a tight embrace.

The couple spent the rest of the evening basking in the glow of their love and discussing their future together. They knew that there would be challenges ahead, but they were ready to face them together.

As they lay in bed that night, holding each other close, Aisha knew that she had found her soulmate in Fatima. She couldn't wait to start their new life together and build a future filled with love, acceptance, and happiness.

The Ranch

"Seize her!", the sheriff's men grabbed her by her hands.

"Wait, no please don't do that." She cried out.

"She had stolen from us, she must be taken to the cell room but first, she would be delivered by the cleric and then locked up in a room. To take off all those evil spirits locked in her body." Heather said.

"What? Mother no! I don't understand." There was a quiver in Faye's voice.

"Take her away." Mr August ordered. And then the Sheriff and some men pulled Jolene by her hands. Faye tried to fight back but she was overpowered by the men and so she fell to the ground in tears.

"What she has done, I have done too. So you need to take me with you." Faye cried out.

"Please, take me with you."

The squeals of the train wheel rolling on the track had made it futile for the passengers to sleep during the day. And by dusk, its high-pitched whistles were like a forlorn call, incessantly vibrating the stapes in their inner ears.

Jolene leaned on the cosy upholstery seat resting her head on the cold glass with her grey hat over her face. It was her dad's favourite hat, one of his things she could keep. The puffy end of the three-layered bustle silk dress she had on, had not made it any easier to get on the train, so she had lost her Fanchon bonnet when she had struggled her way into it.

She had not thought that she would get to embark on a far journey all by herself before her next birthday when she would be eighteen. She never liked to travel, only on rare occasions when she would travel with her parents for certain activities in other cities. But now, she had no choice, she didn't want to wait for another month before Mr Andrew, her father's closest friend, would come to take her along. She had received a letter from Mr Andrew a few days ago, informing her about his long-lasting engagements that will last him for a month. And so, he had sent her some money to embark on the journey down to Houston.

Jolene had never imagined that she would move away from Kansas city or settle in the second-class compartment on the train. She had always preferred the plush velvet seat that could be converted into snug sleeping berths, in the first class compartment couch. But she had unconsciously run out of money after a quarter of the funds she had gone with were presumed stolen at the beginning of her trip. She would classify her journey to Houston as an arduous one.

The two days in the train had given Jolene a rumbling stomach as she had only had yeast bread for these days and a searing head pain from the rustling sound of the engine of the train, and the constant roaring laughter of the hoarse voice from the men in the train.

"Are we there yet?"

"Are you there yet?" Jolene asked the skinny man sitting opposite her.

He slowly opened his eyes, rubbing the back of his palm on his eyes.

"Hurray! She speaks. You haven't said anything ever since we left Kansas. I never thought you would say a word." He scratched off the twirled bushy outcrops moustache on his chin with his thin lips now stretched in a wry smile.

She looked away tweaking the edges of the cotton gloves she had on.

"How far are we to Houston?" She asked shyly.

"Just a couple of hours more and we would be off the train. I noticed you've been alone all this while, are you travelling alone?" He asked. "Yes, I am". She hung her head watching her hands

"A girl your age shouldn't be travelling alone. Where are your parents?" He asked, staring at her, she lowered her brows pulling them closer with her lips drawn downwards which gave her a gloomy look. She tried to speak but she was choked up in her words and so she looked away through the window of the moving train, watching the hazy view of the trees and the road. "There is more yeast bread in the leather bag, you can have some of it if you are hungry". He said.

But she didn't shift her gaze until he went back to his nap.

She leaned back just as he did, but she didn't place the hat over her face again, it was just the silk scarf that was wrapped around her neck. She watched the flare of black smoke puffed from the stack into the air by the steam engine, race across the window. The foggy dark mist that filled the sky was continuously been waved away by the fast-moving train. The hissing from the steam engine had become loud as there were now fewer noises from the men. Gradually, her eyelids fell close until she drifted into a nap just like the skinny man did.

●●●

Finally, the wheels of the train came to a halt. The blazing midday sun shone relentlessly on her white pale skin as she got off. She walked with the square large boxes locked in her hands hustling her way through the crowd down to a street flooded with thick brown sand. The road shimmered in the heat of the midday sun which planted beads of sweat on her face. She struggled with the sole of her shoes which were half buried in the hot sand when she walked.

With her high cheeks that fitted her oval face, Jolene was an elegant growing woman, modest and restrained. She had a sculpted figure which was twine thin, her impeccable complexion with dark hair in artfully placed curls and ringlets.

Her father had said countless times about giving her out to Mr Thomas, the rich sailor for marriage as soon as she was done with her twentieth birthday. She had imagined her life with Thomas, a British sailor, that usually held a stick of cigarette in between his lips, puffing out smoke from his mouth whenever he spoke. He had straight-lined hair on his upper lips he usually called a moustache. Jolene had wondered what being a wife to a sailor would look like, if she would travel across the oceans with him, go on different adventures, get seasick and feed on poisonous creatures just as she had heard Thomas tell her father about one of his trips when he had visited on a Sunday afternoon. She had thought it would be wonderful until her mother had told her that as a wife, she would not sail with Thomas unless it was extremely necessary.

She walked on for a while in bold steps holding the boxes beside her. There was an increasing sound coming from a distance, it sounded just like the hoof of a horse thumping on the ground, like a low-tuned gallop and neighs of a horse approaching from far away. As the noise got closer to Jolene, she could now hear the screech of the rubber tires from a carriage or a wagon she couldn't tell which it was as it was still a mile away. But she could see the figure of a man mounted on top of the horse's back.

"A horse, that could be a horse." She muttered

" I'd wave it down, I pray it's a kind stranger." She said, gasping for breath as the sun had drained her of her strength. The neckline of her blue dress was now soaked in her sweat and the marking of sweat showed from the back. She stopped by the roadside in a field of dried hay waiting until the horse and the rider came close enough, she waved to the stranger and so he pulled over.

"Hey, mister." She called out to the stranger on the horse. She could see now as it was a brown-coated horse that was attached to the carriage. It seemed he was transporting some goods to town. As they were nearly stuffed with folded clothing materials.

"Would you give me a ride downtown, please? I come from a far journey and I am tired and hungry."

"What are you doing on the long road in this harsh weather? You should be home with your mother, helping with some chores. There may be some bandits lurking around. Where are you headed?"

"I'm going to Houston town, Mr August Morgan's ranch, it's just a bit further, down the road I presume, and the scorching sun is eating me up alive," Jolene said hopefully.

"Oh, I know Mr Andrew's ranch. It's one of the largest ranches in town. The sun's rays are only good for drying the hays but not the skin. Well, I can't say no to a pretty damsel. I'd take you there." He said, she forced out a smile as the blazing sun reflected on her face.

"Hop in, you can push the goods in there aside." Said the man riding the horse. With the strands of wrinkled flesh underneath his eyes. He had a long white beard and thin lips that barely covered his teeth, with a premolar missing from the side.

"Thank you, Mister. You are so kind". She replied to his kind gesture with a smile. Then she climbed onto the carriage, with the metal boxes placed on her lap. Looking through the carriage, the gallops of the horse raised the thick brown dust into the air. She sat still with her legs together and both hands resting on the metal boxes that she placed on her legs. She moved her eyes away from the road and caught the man's eyes on her. He had been moving his gaze backwards occasionally. She straightened out her dress for a while and then adjusted the neckline of her dress, placing the scarf around her neck properly. She watched him, not taking her eyes off him, she knew he watched her and she feared what he might have in mind. But with his fray arms and squeezed-out skin, she knew he had not much strength left in him.

As they rode along, she saw the men of the town_ tall, lanky men with their cowboy hats, mounted on their horses. Some with stern looks and those in pairs laughed out loud, so that she could hear them from the distance. The few women she saw had large baskets in their grasp, with their dresses mostly made of linen and cotton and didn't have many layers like the one they wore in Kansas. She knew she was closer to the town and then she began to imagine life in Houston. Being on the ranch, living with ranchers and her new family, she wanted to go to school to learn how to write and not just walk on the farm. She didn't want to learn French and teach in schools just like her mother had wanted, she wanted something more, to be an explorer. She wanted to be a writer, to go places and read out her poems and even get them published. She had written out a dozen poems but her father had thrown them all in the fire saying that the poems were demonic and not from God. She had stopped writing a few years and had only started a couple of months ago.

Soon, the horse stopped and she peeped through to the man who turned backwards already staring at her.

"This is it. The Morgan's". He said and she stepped out of the carriage.

"Thank you." She forced out a smile.

The Morgan's residence was a huge ranch, surrounded by a low-levelled fence made from a stack of woods. There was a building in the middle, enclosed by the large fields of rice farms. Besides the farm, was a stable of horses and a farmhouse of cattle and other farm animals. As she walked in through an opening of the fence, she sighted a lady hanging some white sheets on the clothesline. She was a little above average, slim and slender looking, with her hair all packed into a bonnet. She wore a dress with a semi-full skirt not as full as the one Jolene had on, she saw Jolene as soon as she walked into the fence.

"Jolene, oh child we have been waiting so long for your arrival". She walked towards her holding her in a tight hug. Then she grabbed her boxes off her hand and moved forward to press her lips on her cheek.

"I never wanted August to let you come here all alone. But I'm glad you could make it...My name is Heather, I'm August's wife. I know you wouldn't probably remember me, you were just a child when I first saw you. Now you are such a grown woman."

"Thank you, Mrs August."

"How was the journey?"

"It was a bit burdensome and punishing."

"No wonder you look pale and hungry. Come in, and I'd make you some porridge and set warm water for your bath. You rig of old train smoke and musky dust. You must be really tired". Heather said.

"You have a lovely home". Jolene said as she walked into it. The house was warm and smelled of custard and coffee. The living room had a large wooden shelf with large books carefully arranged in it.

"Thank you. Let me show you around". The wooden floor of the house creaked out loud when they walked in.

"I'd take this in for you." Mrs August took the boxes and left Jolene in the living room.

Jolene walked close to the shelf, she ran her hands across the books, they were dust free. She pulled out one of the books from the stack of books on the shelf.

"Who are you?" Jolene was startled and turned to the dulcet voice that sounded like a sweet songbird. And then, their eyes met at the first instance, Jolene glancing up from staring at the pages of the book and the girl just coming out from the inner rooms as she rested her eyes on Jolene. She was tall with glossy skin, her long figure sat well on her thin-wafer waist. She had a white flowing dress that held her loosely, with her hands around her. Her hazel brown eyes sparkled with the rays of the light.

Jolene could not look away, she heard her repeat a statement she had made when she came in but she still didn't look away. She stood there speechless with her mind preoccupied with loads of expressions. Then Jolene saw her walk slowly towards the bookshelf, she heard her heart flutter to catch up with the moment that had passed by and felt the skin of her face become hot as she got closer and closer.

"I'm...I'm Jolene. I just came in now" She stuttered.

"Faye, Faye...that's my name." She said,

"Faye?" Jolene asked.

"Yes, I was named after a French scholar."

"That's a nice name." Jolene managed to say as her gaze was still fixed on Faye. Then she turned toward the shelf sliding the book back into the shelf.

"I see you like books," Faye said.

"Yes, I do. I used to read a lot of books back in Kansas. My dad was a scholar and so, he had a lot of books. My favourites are the poets and documentaries of other centuries. I do want to become a writer."

"A writer?"

"Yes, a poet. I write some poems sometimes."

"Come with me." Faye pulled Jolene along into a room that looked like a study room with other larger bookshelves and lots of books. It looked more like a mini library than a study room.

The cosiness of the study room was bowled over by the thin cold air that seemed to have come to stay. Jolene stood by a corner in between shelves, stacked with books that have been through a life of their own. As Faye showed her around, Jolene held a book in her grip moving her eyes to some words that she giggled at the old fairy-tale joke. She lingered longer in the romance and thriller aisles. Engulfing the sweet smell of romance and potentially having to feel the thrills from the thrillers. She had come to find the aura of being around books rather appealing that she spends more time with them. She would find herself scanning through all the angles of the bookshelves whenever she was in her dad's study room, with her neck tilting to positions, yearning to find a book that lurked around in an obscure corner wishing to be found.

Jolene had found her adventurous search in her supposed knowledge land worthwhile, as she strolled around picking out books till they now had a whole stack in her hands, It rested well in her grip.

"Wow, this is magnificent. Why do you have this in your home?". Jolene asked.

"My dad is also a scholar and was also the librarian in the city."

"I feel like this is where I belong."

"Why do you like books so much? I find them a bit boring, especially these old editions." Faye asked.

"For all my years reading, I have always found the older editions to be better." Jolene began.

"I have this feeling that the older the edition, the closer I am to hear the real words of the author, and not some perfectly polished voice of recent scholars. Have you ever imagined reading the first edition of Johnathan Swift, Gulliver's Travel? Or better still the manuscripts. Having the smell of those inks rush down your nose as you flip through the pages. Feeling the hardness of the wove paper in your hands. And laughing to those savage words". Jolene said moving forward and resting her eyes on the book she had in her hands.

"See this? Philosophy of Science is quite an eye-opener, I wonder what hidden words Thomas Kuhn has in there. Original editions are like gems to me. Precious, rare and unique."

"I have never thought of books that way." Faye chuckled. Jolene gazed at her, her eyebrows were blonde with a perfect arch curving around her forehead, and they matched her blonde hair and blonde freckles that were as white as a ball of new wool. Her lips were pale pink, full and supple. And full of wise words, Jolene thought.

"You should put those back." Faye moved closer, taking the pile of books off her hands. Jolene noticed her fragrance for the first time. A tint of roses in lavender oil, perhaps she had oiled her hair with it.

"I see you guys have met. Faye, you know you shouldn't be in here." Heather stood by the door of the study room leaning her shoulders on the frame of the door.

"I'm sorry mother." Faye walked out as Jolene followed her behind.

"Go and prepare the table for supper. Your father will be home soon."

After the evening meal, Jolene lay on one of the bunk beds in the room. She would be sharing a room with Faye, but Faye hadn't retired to bed yet. The lamp was dim, Jolene retrieved a small book from within the depths of her box and began reading through it, and then she got a quill and ink. She sat by the table and began writing down a poem, humming to a tune that rang in her head. On the paper she began to write down:

The blonde lady, her skin birthed clean and perfectly polished. The shrills in her voice showed how pure her soul is. All angels have blonde hair, that's what the cleric said. I do not doubt him now because I have met you. You have a lustrous head of shining hair, I wonder why I can't take you off my mind. What I feel is strange and in a kind of way I love it. I have always been called weird but in the short hours I have known you, you have made me normal. Your thoughtful hazel eyes had made me flutter and when you smiled at me I never wanted the thrills in my belly to cease.

"What have you written?" Faye's voice startled her and so she hid the page underneath her palm.

"It's just a poem." She said moving slowly away from the chair.

"Can I see it?" She asked, walking closer as she gently took the book off, Jolene. Jolene saw her hazel eyes again, she watched them move with the words on the page she had written the poem. Jolene watched her eyes change into a smile now, brightened. Somehow, the colour of the fire had made her eyes brown.

"You write beautifully. How do you get to write like this? Where do your thoughts come from?" Faye asked.

"They aren't my thoughts. These are my feelings and I don't usually lie about them." Jolene said, staring directly into her eyes now. Faye stared back for a while and then looked away.

"I should rest now." Jolene watched her walk over to her bed. And so she turned back to the table staring at the dark thick ink in the ink bottle. She didn't know what Faye had truly thought about what she had written and if she had loved it. She wasn't sure and with the uncertainty, she tore out the page from the book and folded it. Then she walked over to the metal box and hid it beneath her dresses before she retired to her bed. She watched Faye's back that was half tucked into the blanket and her lips raised in a smile before dozing off to sleep.

•••

The chirping birds sat at the edge of the window in the bright morning. Jolene got off the mattress, she didn't find Faye in the room. But she found a piece of note on the table.

"Didn't think you would know the route to this place," Faye said smiling. She held a sickle and a bag that she had taken off the stalk of the rice plant one after the other.

"Your note gave you up," Jolene replied, she found Mrs August with a wide hat holding the same tools.

"Good morning Mrs August."

"Jolene, how was your first night here? Hope you had a good night's rest?" She asked.

"Yes, I did." Jolene walked over to the basket of tools taking off a knife and a bag to a rice plant. She cut out a bud and some of the seeds fell off leaving the stack bending over.

"Hey, that's not how it's done." Faye walked over.

"If you do that, you'd waste the seeds." She said,

"I'm sorry, I don't know how to do this," Jolene said, dropping the knife back on the basket as she stepped away.

"This is how it is done," Faye took the knife to the rice stack and Jolene moved closer, "Take, hold it," Faye held Jolene's hands against hers on the knife.

"You'd use your middle finger, and hold the stem firmly against the metal," They were so close that Jolene could feel her breath on her skin. It was warm and gentle, caressing the hairs on her skin, she could now breathe in the lavender oil on her hair. Jolene moved her eyes from the rice stalk resting it on Faye.

"And then cut off from the plant itself, like this." Faye pulled it out from the stem into the bag she held around her waist. Faye had been neck deep in what she was doing that she had not noticed her eyes on her, just then, she turned to find Jolene's eyes on her. And for the first time, Faye noticed her eyes, they were grey, colourless and yet dominant as the sun.

"You should....you should try it."

"No, I can't destroy another plant." Jolene refused.

"I will be here with you, all the way through," Faye said, handing the knife to Jolene who sluggishly took it off her grasp. She began working on the stalk and as she did, the knife slipped and gave her a minor cut, "Ouch!" she jerked flinging it on the ground.

"I'm so sorry. Let me see it." Faye held Jolene's finger and pressed it with her thumb applying pressure on it.

"Does it hurt?" She asked.

"Not anymore. Where do you learn to do that?"

"Mother used to be a nurse. You shouldn't work with the knife again."

"No, I'm fine. I'd still work. You just have to show me how it should be done again." Jolene said.

"I won't ".

"But why? You are a great tutor." Jolene smiled.

"You didn't pay attention. I caught you staring at me."

"I love staring at you." Faye looked up into her eyes again and then to her lips, she still held Jolene's finger in her hands. They stood staring for a while.

"What's going on here?" Heather's voice startled the girls as they both jerked and turned towards her.

"I was just demonstrating the harvesting procedure to Jolene," Faye said and returned to the rice stalk she was working on.

"We should hurry before the summer sun gets to its peak." Heather stood for a while watching the girls before she went back to work.

"So you have never worked on a rice farm before?" Faye asked.

"Yes, there weren't many ranches back in Kansas."

The local racecourse was a flat track open space of dirt turf. The day's sporting activity wasn't the usual horse racing long-distance competition. It was one of the few seasons where they had hurdles perfectly arranged around a certain distance for the church steeple race. Here, the racers would jump over the hurdles during the race where the first to go over the last hurdle, will be declared the winner.

There were a few men around the open space with the jockeys already mounted on the horse's back. Richard, one of the jockeys, stood beside the other competitors who were already mounted on their horses. He seemed to be ready to compete as he had his silks and boots but his horse had not arrived yet.

"Mr August!" Richard called out to Mr August who approached him from a distance holding the cord that was tied around the neck of the grey horse. He walked towards the direction of Richard whose hands were already waving towards him.

"Mr August, I'm over here."

"Sorry I had delayed, Lisa got to take in more water for this ride." Mr August tapped the torso of the horse as he got closer to Richard.

"I hope she got a tank full because the race is about to begin and I wouldn't want to lose this race." Richard hopped on the back of Lisa and stood in line with the rest of the competitors. They were about eight jockeys waiting for the sound of the gunshot to begin the race.

The church steeple race has been practised in the town for over a decade. Young lads would get their horses prepared from the beginning of the year to July when they would get into the competition to compete. The winner would be awarded and appointed a leadership position among their peers. Richard Darwin the son of Matthew Darwin, the town local sheriff had earlier purchased Lisa when she was just a foal from Mr August. But he had instructed him to look after the horse, preparing it for the day of the competition.

The race began with the firing of the ruffle gun. The jockeys rode their horses, controlling the speed with a whip slash on the back of the horse. Richard had always been skilful on the back of any horse. He rode faster than most of the other men, jumping hurdles and landing steadily. Closer to the finish line, he was in the second position and with an extra whip on the back of Lisa, he got ahead and ended as the winner. There were loud cheers from some of his friends and family. His father only smiled at him and rode off on the back of the horse he had been on when he had come to watch the race of his son. But before he rode off, he walked over to Mr August who had been watching the race all the while.

"How do you do?". His voice was just as hoarse as his appearance.

"How do you do?" They extended their arms in a handshake. That was a good race. Your son earned it and Lisa is a fast horse."

"Yes, he is great with horses. But I do think it is time for him to be more serious as he is now a man. What do you think?"

"Well, that would be a good idea but I won't be the one to tell you how to treat your child."

"I don't need you to. I already know what to do about that, I would only want your approval."

"What do you mean?" Mr August narrowed his eyes.

"I would tell you, but we have to meet in a different environment. Have a nice day Mr August. See you soon."

Mr August was a bit appalled by the words of Mr Matthew. He watched him ride off till he could no longer see his back or the horse again.

"Mr August, did you see that? I was good out there and she is a really fast horse."

"Yes, she is." Mr Andrew took the cord from his grip on Richard.

"Where is my father? I thought I saw him standing over here."

"Yes yes, he just rode off a couple of minutes ago."

•

By dusk, Mr August went to the city tavern. Mr Mathew sat by a table with a mug in front of him.

"I thought I would find you here." Mr August walked closer to him.

"Once in a while, a man does need to cool off with a mug of whisky." Mr Mathew chuckled.

"The Blaze tavern is a better spot for a good whisky."

"I doubt that. The blaze tavern is for the little lads. Richard and his friends could be there right now celebrating his victory as the fastest horse racer. Drinking in some tequila with the whores warming their bed. He would never be a man without a wife."

"Hmm, your words got me wondering." Mr August said.

"Yes. I would want Richard to take your daughter as a wife. She is grown and fit to be married and he is ready."

"I knew this day would come when I would have to give her up for marriage. And I am glad you asked. But I would want her to finish French school first. She will be done by winter."

"That wouldn't be a problem at all. Thank you, Mr August, I would be waiting for your feedback. Speak to your daughter."

•••

The hot summer sun had finally set and the night had come. The city was mostly quiet and peaceful with the breeze nudging the edges of the curtains in the room. It brought in the cool breeze making the room cold.

"Come lie with me. We could cuddle and make ourselves warm." Faye watched Jolene shrink underneath her blanket. Jolene trotted over and Faye wrapped her arms around her

"You aren't writing tonight."

"My head is chilly and my mind is blank," Jolene said. Faye moved her hands over to Jolene's forehead resting them there. Jolene shut her eyes feeling the warmth of her palms on her head.

"How does that feel?"

"Warm", Jolene smiled.

"Why do you have a blank mind?"

"It is one of those cold nights when I can't take the cruelty of this world off my mind. The times when I wish I could have done something to save my parents."

"It's not your fault that they drowned Jol."

"Drowned? Where did you hear that from?" Jolene moved away from her grip and turned to face her.

"My parents told me how the harsh weather had drowned the ship."

"They didn't drown. They were killed by some bandits."

"That's terrible Jol. I'm sorry about that. But why will my parents lie to me?"

"Maybe, they were just trying to protect you."

Jolene still held her hands together, folding as she lay.

"Do you still feel cold?"

"Yes, the blankets aren't made of wool, but the warmth from your arms has helped a little."

"What would the warmth from my whole body do?" Faye sat upwards, and Jolene moved her eyes with her as she got off the bed. Then she took the sleeves from her shoulders one after the other till the white silk night dress fell off to the ground revealing her graceful body. The yellow light reflected on her white skin giving her a golden look. The nipples of her breast pointed at Jolene. She was beautiful with the arch of her curves perfectly carved out. Jolene couldn't take her eyes off her body. Faye climbed back on the bed underneath the blanket and held Jolene again. Jolene felt her body pressed against hers. Feeling her glossy slender skin. She felt some sort of emotional warmth that welcomed her soul deeply. She was blessed to be in the arms of the sweet grace of stunning beauty. Soon, she could smell her lavender oil all over her skin. She had never felt this fleeting care and affection or connection for anyone.

"How do you feel now?"

"I write words but you have made me run short of them. I can't explain what I feel, I know it's beyond words. But this is more than I asked for." Jolene smiled.

"I'm glad you are okay now," Faye said, still holding her.

"What do you want to do?" Jolene asked.

"I want to become a teacher and a good wife."

"I mean what do you want to do?"

Faye exhaled forcefully and pulled away her arms around Jolene.

"No one has ever asked me this question. Apart from swimming in the lake, I want to be a Jockey. Race the fastest horse in the field and win races. I have always dreamt about that. But mother said we are only allowed to have fantasies."

"Ride a horse? That's so brave of you. I have never really ridden on one. Have you?"

"Yes, I used to sneak out to the stables and ride on my horse when we were both little. I taught myself how to ride."

Jolene's eyes broadened in surprise, "You have a horse?"

"I used to. Her name was Lisa, and she was my favourite but my dad sold her off even when he knew I loved her. He said women don't ride horses. So he sold her to the Sheriff. But he didn't take Lisa with him.

She is still in the stables so I only go out to see her sometimes but I can never ride her."

"That's unfair." Jolene sighed.

"No, it's not, we aren't allowed to do a lot of things so we would be able to produce children without complications." Faye forced out a smile.

"I know what we will do tomorrow."

"What would we do?"

"Get some sleep Fay, get some rest."

They lay cuddling in each other's arms till Faye fell asleep, then Jolene pecked her on her forehead and crawled out of the bed, covering her up in the blanket. She went over to the box, retrieved the book and walked on tiptoes to the chair so she wouldn't wake Faye up. She soaked the quill in the ink and began to write:

Tonight was blissful, a night I would not forget in a thousand years. Like Cleopatra, you are a goodness of beauty. Even in the darkest of the night, the golden light on your skin sparkled. Your supple skin on mine was subtle. Now I still smell your sweet lavender on my skin, at least I have a part of you on me. I will not wash it away, not now; not ever. I thought I was brave until I met you, I wonder why we are trapped in this world. You know we do not belong here. Tomorrow, I will take you to where you most desire so we can walk your dreams together.

Jolene was all smiles by the time she was done writing. As she closed the book to put it away, her elbow hit the ink bottle off the table and a bit of it spilt down on the floor. She wiped it with a piece of clothing and only a bit of it went off then she flung the piece of clothing underneath the bed bunk where she dropped the book.

It was the beginning of fall, the dry ground was littered with withered leaves from the white oak trees in the woods. Faye led Jolene through the woods to the boardwalk of the lake which had green ferns surrounding it. The insects of the woods hummed around the petals of the flowers in line with the chirping birds.

"This is where I come to sometimes when I want to get away from home and clear my head. I don't think anyone has been here in years. I love to hear the birds sing and see the airwaves of the branches of the tree, feeling the breeze on my skin." Faye twirled and turned with the leaves suspended in the air by the wind.

"It's so peaceful. Why do the flamingos keep perching on the water?" Jolene asked, moving closer to the end of the boardwalk.

"I think they pick out the worms from the water. That's what they eat."

"Well, I hope the warms wouldn't mind seeing an uncovered damsel." Jolene pulled out the drawstrings from the neckline of her dress.

"What are you doing?" Faye broadened her eyes.

"I want to get in the water." Jolene pulled out the rest of her dress and plunged into the lake.

"But that's not ethical. Someone could be watching us."

"You said no one has been here in years. Wow! I love the feel of this water on my skin. You should come in here."

"I don't think I can." Faye stuttered.

"This is what you have always wished for. You are a brave and bold woman. It's okay, you can trust me." Jolene started watching her. Faye stood for a while then began to take off her dress. Then she put the tip of the toe of her left foot first in the water and then Jolene helped her in.

"I can't believe I'm doing this. It's so cold. I hope no one is watching. I'm so scared." Faye began to scamper, turning her head around in fear.

"Hey, hey", Jolene held her in the water and turned to face her. "It's okay. It's just me and you. No one else, nothing else matters right now." She let out a smile and Faye returned it with a warmer smile. Jolene began to flap her arms and legs soon, she began to swim in the lake, and Faye joined her. But Faye was a better swimmer than Jolene.

Jolene began with the first splash of water and Faye followed in a short while, they were both sloshing and sprinkling the water on each other in the shallow end of the lake. They teased each other's hair giggling and chuckling at every action.

Shortly, they were out of the water still in their merry laughter that they didn't know would be short-lived.

"I can still feel the coolness in my bones." Jolene chuckled, straightening out her dress.

"This was magnificent. I haven't felt this excitement before. Thank you, Jol for coming into my life." Faye said moving to Jolene, she took her hands in hers and they looked directly at each other. Then, Faye moved closer and she pressed her body together against Jolene. Warmth blossomed in Jolene's chest, sparks igniting as Faye leaned in close, lips brushing together. Jolene's eyes were half closed and so were Faye's. She wanted to open them, she wanted to get a better look at those hazel eyes and pink freckles. She had this feeling that this might never happen again and so she savoured every inch of it. Faye felt her heartbeat thud, the dizzying smell of Jolene's peachy fragrance overwhelmed her. They stared into each other's eyes when they pulled away from each other.

"I'm sorry. I got carried away." Faye apologized, She didn't know why she had kissed Jolene but it felt perfect as it left butterflies dancing in her belly.

"No, don't be." Jolene moved closer again, she nudged her nose against Faye's and their lips felt sleepy together again.

•••

Richard sat with his closest friend, Arthis They shared a bottle of whiskey. Arthis moved about demonstrating like the clerics conducting a sermon.

"I wonder what clerics take whiskey. You still haven't told me why you chose the church." Richard said.

"The church is a spiritual place, I spend more time there. That's why I can't wait to be done with the theological school so I can finally become a cleric."

"When is your due date?" Richard lolled to the chair.

"By winter."

"Winter?! I'd be getting married by winter. And I wouldn't want you to miss my wedding."

"True. I forgot. You haven't told me anything about this lady. She must have caught your eye. I mean, you have never agreed to marry anyone, but have agreed to marry her. That should count for something. Tell me about her."

"I don't know much about her. But she is a young and pretty damsel. Her name is Faye. I can't wait to have her as my bride. She would warm my bed and cook meals for me." Richard grinned, pouring out some of the whiskey into the glass.

●●●

In the early days of October, Jolene joined Faye in the French school. She did not like the idea but she was happy to go anywhere with Faye. In the morning, they would go for the classes and would sneak out to the lake where no one would see them or an abandoned cabin where they would spend time together. The girls had been together in the cabin with their lips locked together when the cabin door was flung open, it was a stern-looking man in his mid-forties who had seen them. He appeared to be drunk as he staggered on his feet. They had fled out through the cabin window before he could see their faces or so they thought. The moon was already up when they got back home.

As they walked into the house, they met the stern-looking man in the living room with Mr August and his wife. The couples seemed not to be pleased by the sight of the girls as they held their faces in anger and scorn.

"Mother, what's going on?" Faye asked as they all looked at them with a look of disgust.

"Is this man telling the truth?" Heather asked.

"What truth?" Faye was in disarray.

"Did you lay with a woman?" Mr August asked.

"This man said he had seen you with a lady in a cabin. Is this true?"

"No, father. I was not in the cabin with anyone." Faye tried to keep her voice from trembling.

"But this man here says otherwise."

"Did he see the face of the lady he claimed to have seen me with?" Faye asked confidently, avoiding the eyes of the man. They stalled for a while looking at each other.

"No, he didn't."

"Then it wasn't me father. Do not believe this man over your child. Perhaps he is drunk and seeing things."

Jolene only stood beside Faye without saying a word her heartbeat tripled and for the first time she felt scared. But they didn't know that this was just the beginning of their unseemly love tale.

"Jolene, you can go inside. Faye sit down. I think it's time we told you."

"What are you talking about? What do you want to tell me?"

Jolene walked into the inner room. She couldn't have guessed what they were about to relay to Faye but whatever it was might be pretty serious. She walked over to the bed bunk underneath it where she retrieved her book. She began to write:

This was the first time I was scared for my life because you are a part of it now. In the past, I could have cared less. I had always wished to be swallowed by the sea and buried in the deepest parts of the ocean after my parents were taken from me. I do not want to leave you in this part of the world alone. We kissed, oh yes! We kissed. Your kiss has changed me. It made me feel whole again. Who would want something that beautiful to suddenly end?

I fear for my life and I fear for yours too. I want to protect you in every way. The people would not understand what we share. But I do not wish to hide in corners and crannies when I'm with you. I want the world to know us. Yes! I do.

Jolene jerked from the loud thud she heard from the room door. Faye flung herself on the bed drowning in her tears.

"What is it, my love? What have they said to you?" Jolene moved over to the bed wrapping her arms around her.

"I do not wish to marry him."

"Marry who?"

"I do not wish to marry the sheriff's son." Faye sniffed in the mucus that was running down her nose.

"What do you mean?" Jolene's voice trembled.

"Mother and father had agreed for me to marry him. By the end of the year, I would be his wife." Faye said out loud in her teary edge voice. Jolene moved away a bit gasping in the air as she heard the words of Faye.

"I do not wish to be married to him."

"Come here." Jolene leaned closer to her again as she rested on her lap. Then she ran her fingers into her hair and began humming a song. It was a tune her mother had taught her to sing whenever she was ever scared.

"Let us go on a ride on the back of Lisa, I saw the stable boy put her back in the stable." Faye wiped off the tears from the corners of her eyes.

"Do you want to do that now? The moon is out already."

"Yes, it is a perfect time. I want to dance under the moon with you. At least now I'm not yet married. If you love me, you would come with me." Jolene smiled at her and they set off for Lisa. They sneaked out of the house carefully closing the doors to prevent the creaking of the hinges to wake up the household.

They went to the stables, took the keys from the pocket of one of the stable boys who was fast asleep and then they freed Lisa taking her into the woods.

Faye flung herself on the back of the horse and stretched out her hands to get Jolene but Jolene only moved backwards tilting her head.

"We can't come out here and you don't get to ride her with me. Together, remember?"

Jolene nodded with a wry smile and then took Faye's hand as she sat on Lisa's back.

"Hold on to me closely."

"Hiya!" Faye beat the side of Lisa's torso and the horse began to run. At first, Jolene was scared, she kept her eyes shut and gripped fearfully on Faye. But soon, she began to open her eyes gradually and let go of the rims of Faye's dress. It was dark but they could still see the paths in the woods as the moon illuminated their way.

"You are such a cowgirl! This is the best night of my life." The girls kept their arms apart like they were about to fly and felt the cool night breeze run to their faces. They got off Lisa and began to dance playfully in the woods. They danced around the fire they put on. They screamed at top of their voices to the woods as no one could hear them. But they didn't know that perhaps it would be their last night together in Houston.

They fell on the floor giggling as they faced the stars.

"It's a beautiful night. Look at all those stars." Faye pointed to the sky.

"Yea it is. But not as beautiful as you are tonight." Jolene turned towards Faye, they kissed passionately under the moon. They breathed heavily as they shared their breaths feeling the thuds of each other's heartbeats fumbling to take off each other's clothes.

By morning, the girls lay spooned on the bare ground with their dresses tossed aside. The fire had gone off but the dark smoke still went up into the air. The men in the surrounding had seen the dark smoke from the forest and had come into the forest to check out who had put out a fire. As they drew closer, the dry leaves rustled under the sole of their shoes. The rustle from the leaves began to wake up the girls. They had stayed up all night and had fallen asleep as soon as it was dawn.

"What sorcery is this?!" The first man yelled as he got to see the girls. They managed to open their weary eyes to find them surrounded by a group of men.

"What are you ladies doing here? What did you girls come in here to do?" The man asked.

"Faye!" Richard called out, "What is this?"

"Do you know them?"

"Yes, Faye is my bride-to-be, Mr August's daughter and the other lady is Jolene, she has been in town for a while now. I need to see Mr August." Richard walked back, and Faye rushed towards him.

"Richard! Richard! Please hear me out. You can't tell anyone about this."

"Oh, I can and I will. I would like to know what the town feels about this after I relayed this to my father and your parents." He threatened, he shoved Faye's grip away from his shoulders.

"Please wait! " She cried out running towards him, holding the edges of her dress in her hands. Jolene ran behind her and she too was terrified.

"Is this a one-time thing?" Richard turned towards her.

"I...I"

"I guess not." He said and got on his horse. Faye and Jolene could not find Lisa where they had tied her to a tree trunk and so they began to walk back home on foot. As they walked through the town, they could see the eerie stares from the rest of the town. It was appalling how words could get to the whole town before they could even get home.

They could hear the people talk about them, and some of them called them different names.

As they walked in through the door, Mr August, his wife and the cleric were already seated in the living room. They seemed to be talking about something personal as they talked in low tune. Jolene and Faye didn't find Richard and his friends in there and so they guessed that he had not arrived yet, but what was the cleric doing in their home at that hour?

The way they looked at the girls when they walked in, it was difficult to detect if they had known what had happened even if half the town was already aware of them.

Jolene sighted the black book on the table, she walked over to it, snatching it off the table.

"Faye, she led you into this. I know she did." Heather began pulling Faye away from Jolene who stood stiff pondering on what had happened.

"You evil child. Did your mother not teach you the right way?" She was staring sternly at Jolene now.

Richard had already dropped in with his friends and had told them what he had seen. Heather had earlier found Jolene's poetry book underneath her bed and so she believed Richard and his friends when they came. They had quickly sent for the cleric as they thought their daughter needed cleansing as she had sinned and Jolene needed to be delivered.

"Mother, I am sorry but I do not want to marry Richard. I love Jolene and I want to be with her."

"Do not speak of love, you know nothing about it, your words are nothing but that of a child." Mr August barked.

August's door was flung open as the sheriff and his men flooded August's living room.

"What's going on here?" Mr August asked as the group of men entered his home. The sheriff walked over to him and puffed out smoke from his mouth as he drew smoke from the pipe.

"Someone stole Lisa from the stables and sold her to a merchant in the next town."

"What?!" Mr August stood in shock.

"And we have found the culprit. We would be taking Jolene here with us."

"Wait, what? I didn't sell Lisa off. We only took her out for a ride, I presumed someone might have taken her."

"With those words, you have just confessed to the accusation."

"Cease her!", the sheriff's men grabbed her by her hands.

"Wait, no please don't do that." She cried out.

"She had stolen from us so she must be taken to jail but first, she would be delivered by the cleric and then locked up in a room. To take off all those evil spirits locked up in her body." Heather said.

"What? Mother no! I don't understand." There was a quiver in Faye's voice.

"Take her away." Mr August ordered. And then the Sheriff and some men pulled Jolene by her hands. Faye tried to fight back but she was overpowered by the men and so she fell to the ground in tears.

"What she has done, I have done too. So you need to take me with you." Faye cried out.

"Please, take me with you."

Heather pulled her away from the men as they took Jolene out.

Faye lay in her bed drowned in her tears, she feared what they might do to Jolene.

"Mother, Jolene does not deserve to be treated that way. She didn't do anything."

"You need to get cleansed and ready for your marriage."

"I do not want to get married."

"That girl has changed you, she has taken away the modesty in you and we will not let that happen. She needs to go away!"

Faye stopped crying for a while and stared at her mother. "Where will she go? She has nowhere to go."

"Get yourself ready, Faye," Heather said and walked out of the room.

It has been over a month, and Faye has not heard anything from Jolene nor has she been let out of the house. She wondered how Jolene was, If she was still alive, thought about what they had done to her. Then she went over to her mother when her father had gone out on a cold afternoon.

"I know Jolene is locked up somewhere here in town. I have concluded. I would only marry Richard if you let Jolene go and then I would not speak of her again. I would love Richard and be a good wife to him."

Heather breathed in deeply and then walked over to Faye moving her hands over her hair.

"You have made the right choice. On the morning of your wedding, we would let Jolene go. But she will be told never to return here again."

"When is my wedding?"

"When you are ready."

"I am ready." Faye stared at her mother for a while and then looked away.

"Then I would talk to your father to speak to the sheriff. I am proud of you."

●●●

In a locked room, Jolene sat on a small bed by the wall with the quill and ink by her side. She dipped the quill in the ink and then began to write:

Faye, I heard from one of the guards that you chose to marry Richard just so I would be set free. I have always thought you courageous and I have never been wrong. This past month I have spent in this cell room, I have had a lot of time to think about everything. Meeting you has been the best part of my life.

With each passing day, I grow cold in this room. Wondering if I will ever see you again to have a taste of your lips that is as soft as the first snowballs. I would be leaving on the day of your wedding and I don't know when that is but any day I am set free again I will know you had made the sacrifice for me.

Whenever you see the lake or Lisa again, then think of me.

Jol.

She tore off the page and folded it then she slipped it under the door to the guard who had promised her that he would have it delivered to Faye before her wedding. She didn't know if she ever received it or if her mother or father had found it and disposed of it.

It was snowing when she was let out of the cell room.

"You can go now, these are your boxes and the train leaves in an hour. If I were you, I would begin the long walk down to the train station before the train leaves." The guard said.

Jolene began the long walk down to the train station. The white balls of snow fell on her skin and her hair but she didn't look back. She basked in the coldness of winter and her teeth gritted in a shiver. She had tried not to think about Faye and all that had happened but she knew it would take so many walks alone to forget about Faye.

"Jol! Jol! Jolene!"

Jolene turned towards the sound of the voice that she heard from a distance.

Who could that be? She wondered. The snowfall had increased since she started the walk down to the train station and so her vision was blurry. She had become weak and needed to rest but the train station was still a few miles down.

"Jolene!" She heard the voice again.

"Faye!" She called out as soon as she could catch a glimpse of the figure running towards her. Her blonde hair flung on her shoulders as she ran. She looked even more pretty in her full white dress. It was made of different layers of chiasmus fabric and silk. The white full dress swept the first layer of the white snow on the ground. She had a brown box in her hands. Jolene dropped the boxes on the ground and spread her arms to catch Faye in them. She was warm and grabbed Jol in a tight hug.

"Jol."

"Faye, what are you doing here? You should be getting married today."

"I couldn't do it. I couldn't marry Richard."

"But...how do you know I'd be here?"

"I got your letter," Faye said.

"And you left your wedding for me?"

"Yes, I had to run away. I cannot stay without you. This past month was terrible. I want to come with you. Explore the world and ride horses. I don't want to be a good wife, at least not now. I discovered the sheriff made up the whole story just to get rid of you and he sold the horse himself. Look, I took the money with me. We can use it to start our life afresh in a new town far away from here." She chuckled.

"You took the sheriff's money."

"Yes, after all, he steals from the people."

"Then we better head to the train station before the sheriff discovers his money is missing."

"Where should we go?" Jolene asked.

"Dakota. I have always wanted to visit there. I wonder what life would be like."

"Then let's go to Dakota." They giggled and held each other's hands as they began the long run to freedom.

What Is Love?

WHAT IS LOVE? L-o-v-e; just four tiny letters. Love; just one simple word. Love, no two people would create the same definition. When it comes to love, the feeling actually had been a mystery to me as I feel like I'm was on this quest to really find true love. Love;. So many different kinds, so many different emotions. I love my mother; I love my decaf mochas; I loved my teddy bear from when I was three; I love the Big Bang Theory; I love to read; I love teaching; I love wearing stockings; I love sex. Yet had I ever felt true love? I don't know. I definitely thought I was in love on a few occasions, but that faded away over time. I love you; Three simple words. I have said them before; I have had them said to me; were they meant sincerely? I like to think so. Were they actually true deep down in their heart? Maybe, I just wasn't sure.

This is my love story. It is a complex, layered and sexually filled story. Will you think it is a true love story? That is up to you, as each defines love as they see it. So don't judge my view of love. It is messy, complicated, and addictive and, yet I think, pure. It wasn't until I was 27 and my best friend for many years announced she was engaged and getting married that I realized I was in love; pure, unconditional love. A love that overwhelms you. It is intoxicating; bewildering; overwhelming; haunting. This is the story of how I found such a love. For me, love equals Mia.

Mia and I were best friends since grade 8. We had almost every class together and graduated together. We both lost our virginity at our grade 12 prom, on a double dare that had become a tradition between us. We would both dare each other to do the same thing. In grade 10 it was to walk up and kiss a nerd; by grade 12 we were daring each other to flash old men, go without underwear during a cheerleading practice, and lastly daring each other to give up our cherries to our respective boyfriends at prom, both of us having turned 18 the month before.

In college the dares got crazier, each one created by me. Mia was psychologically shy, yet when a dare was given the shy facade always seemed to fade away as she also hated to lose.

Anyway I digress; we both got our teaching degrees at the same college. Luckily for us, we also got jobs at the same school; me teaching kindergarten and Mia teaching grade 3. Over the next few years I dated a couple men before strictly dating women. Unfortunately, I had been through a string of women. I broke up with women for many trivial reasons: she had an annoying laugh; she was too high maintenance; she was too low maintenance; her family was crazy; she wasn't intelligent enough for me; she was too intelligent for me; she wasn't good enough in bed; etc... What I realized after the fact is they actually all had the same problem...they were not Mia. Mia, on the other hand, dated a couple guys briefly before falling hard for a decent guy named Scott.

Anyways, life went on and had been very normal, until she announced she was getting married. It shouldn't have been a big deal as they had lived together for two years already and nothing had really changed in our relationship. We still had our weekly girls' night, our occasional dares, our daily phone calls and our constant text messages. Yet, when she gave me the news, something triggered deep inside me. I had this empty feeling and then it was replaced by this overwhelming fear and then it was replaced by something I can't explain. A light bulb went on. It didn't flicker, it shined bright. I was in love with Mia. Not as a friend, not as a sibling; no, I loved her in an 'I want to spend the rest of my life with you' love. It was hard for me to just digest the news that Mia was getting married to someone else, not me.

That night I went to bed alone thinking of the few times we experimented with each other. It started with drunken kissing a few times to tease the boys at the pub, then one time for the boys when I fingered her, on a drunken dare of mine, for their entertainment; on a few occasions we masturbated side by side as we watched some porn and then eventually helped each other reach orgasmic bliss once...just once. I remember how gentle she was and how she found my g-spot, something very few had ever been able to do. In retrospect, that night was so tender, so gentle, and so perfect. Unfortunately, we never were intimate again, nor had we ever talked about that one special night.

Then I reflected on our friendship. I was the outgoing one, while she was more reserved. I was sarcastic funny, while she was quirky funny. I was always the one making the plans, while Mia simply went along with it. I was confrontational, while she avoided it at all costs.

The more I considered Mia and me, the more revelations exploded inside my head. She always let me decide what we did when we went out; she never disagreed with me, even when she clearly didn't agree with me; she always listened to my advice on fashion, make-up, etc.; she began wearing stockings after I suggested that they were sexy (now she always wears them).

As I considered our brief intimate encounters another eye-opener emerged. I was always the initiator, while she was always the follower. When we first masturbated each other it was me who suggested she let me help her out. It was all coming together. The puzzle pieces didn't all fit yet, but the picture was beginning to come into focus. Mia was submissive. I had been with a few submissive women in my past and knew how to manipulate them. If Mia was submissive, which I was pretty sure she was, I could seduce her.

I should note that I am a very attractive woman. I am 5 foot 6, hypnotic hazel eyes, long red flowing hair, small but firm breasts, a perfect tan, an intoxicating smile, a tight ass and luscious legs. I don't mean to sound arrogant, but men and women have been checking me out since I was a teenager.

Mia is also pretty, but in a much more wholesome way. She is more the girl next door type. She is a brunette, with unique crystal blue eyes, large breasts which she often hides behind sweaters, a slightly chunky ass, lips to die for, cute dimples and a smile that sparkles.

Anyways, I fell asleep pondering...did she love me too? Would she have done more with me if I had made a move?

A few things became crystal clear:

1. I loved Mia.

2. I had to stop the wedding.

3. I had to seduce Mia.

I barely slept as I considered by seduction plan.

The next couple of weeks it was simple things. I started hugging her when we saw each other and complimented her every chance I got. The compliments during this time were simple, flattering compliments, things a man would never say. "Oh you painted your nails a new shade of red" or "Those shoes really help showcase your legs," or "Is that a new lipstick? It really makes your lips come to life." Each compliment seemed to perk up Mia.

Then we went bridesmaid dress shopping.

"So what color are you thinking the bridesmaids should wear?" I asked as we arrived at the store.

"I don't know I was thinking green."

"I look amazing in green," I said flirtingly.

"I know it's your favorite color," she responded.

I coyly ask her, "But do I look hot in green?"

She blushed, ever so slightly, as she said with a slight laugh, "Yes, you look hot in green Claire."

I smiled and gave her a big hug. I then whispered in her ear, "You look hot in everything you wear." I then kissed her cheek, something I had started a couple of weeks ago, and we started looking at dresses.

I pointed out a couple nice ones and then headed to try on a nice dark green one that was sexy, yet still wedding appropriate. When I came out to show it off a pretty saleswoman, who looked to be in her early twenties, give or take, was there to assist us. Her name tag said Sophia. I looked in the mirror and asked, "How do I look?"

Mia said, "It looks really good on you."

"You think?" I asked. Taking a long look in the mirror I then said, "This would definitely need stockings."

Mia agreed, "Yes, either black or dark beige."

I looked at Sophia and said, "Do you sell stockings here?"

"Yes," Sophia responded.

I smiled at her, my sexy flirting smile, "Not pantyhose, but thigh high stockings."

Sophia smiled back at me with a similar flirting smile, "Yes ma'am. That is all I wear as well. I would recommend French Coffee."

It was my turn to be impressed. "I have never heard of French Coffee as a colour."

Sophia smiled and said, "Do you like the colour I am wearing?"

"They are very fetching, but they are suntan are they not?" I said.

"Very good. Well French coffee is a darker shade, one that would be perfect with that shade of green. They are a 50s style vintage stocking."

"Can you get me a pair?" I asked.

"Yes ma'am," she responded.

"It's Claire," I said.

"I will get you a pair," she paused smiling coyly at me, "Claire."

As she walked away, I watched her waiting for the look back; as expected, it came with a sly smile. I looked at Mia and said, "What do you think Mia? Think I can seduce her?"

Mia looked at me with a look I could not read. "Well few have ever been able to resist the Claire charm." It should be noted that Mia has seen me seduce many men and women throughout the years.

"You did," I paused, "Well mostly."

Mia blushed, but before I could continue cute little Sophia returned. The brunette handed me a package. Instead of going back to change in the dressing room, I simply opened the package and decided to put them on in front of the two girls I was trying to seduce.

I slid off my three inch pumps and slowly slid a stocking on my tanned legs. I made sure to make eye contact with Sophia as I put on the first stocking. As I put on my second stocking I looked eye to eye with Mia who watched before looking away when she realized I saw her watching. I then looked in the mirror. Pretty Sophia was right. The stockings really showcased both my legs and the dress. My long red hair also was showcased by the dress. I never looked better. I looked at Sophia and said, "Good call, how do I look?"

"You look radiant ma'am, I mean Claire." She said overly friendly.

"Radiant. That is very flattering. Can you bring me a pair of matching heels for this dress?"

"Sure," she said, "A size 6 I assume."

"You are very good at your job Sophia, a size six indeed."

Sophia walked away, her ass swaying perfectly in her tight black skirt.

I winked at Mia as I quickly pulled off my panties and tossed them to Mia. She was startled, but only briefly, as she quickly put them in her purse.

Sophia came back with two shoe boxes and knelt beside me. I lifted my foot up, legs open enough to showcase my shaved pussy, as Sophia slid on the matching green pump, slowly caressing the back of my ankle and calf as she did so. She was a seductress too. Even so, her face gave a startled look as she saw my uncovered cunt. She lingered longer than propriety would allow, before reaching down for the second shoe. As she put the second heel on, she again took a lingering look at my delicious pussy. As she was hypnotically seduced by my appetizing delicacy, I said, "Like what you see?"

She broke her stare and stood up embarrassed and tried to change the topic. "Um, those shoes really work for this outfit ma'am."

I smiled at her and said, "It is Claire dear. Plus you didn't answer my question." I then moved close to her and whispered, "Did you like what you saw."

Her face was red, yet she caught on to the game quickly as she recovered, "Very much so."

"I thought you would," I said and turned to look in the mirror while I winked at Mia who shook her head. "Sophia these are good, but not amazing. What else do you have for me?"

She reached for the other box as I sat back down and lifted up my leg, angled so this time Mia could take a peak as well. Sophia slid off my shoe and replaced it with a sexier pump with a strap that wrapped around my ankle. Sophia took her time putting my shoe on; her gaze rarely leaving mine. When both shoes were on, I checked the mirror and knew instantly this was perfect. I did a twirl and said, "So Sophia, how do I look?"

Sophia walked over to me and said, "Ravishing."

I smiled back, "Thanks Sophia. Mia I think this is the dress and these are definitely the shoes. You think?"

Mia, who was gawking at me quite frankly, responded awkwardly, "Yes, yes, they are perfect."

I turned to Sophia, "We will buy it all Sophia. Can you help me get the dress off please," I asked as I went into the changing room.

Sophia looked back to see if anyone was coming before following me into the room.

As soon as the door was closed, I pushed her against the wall and kissed her passionately. She kissed back with a similar intensity. I broke the kiss eventually and she helped me out of the dress. I kept on the nylons and fingered my pussy quickly before putting my finger at Sophia's lips. She obediently opened her lips and savoured my love juice. I then got dressed and said, "Sophia, I will be at The Pheonix Club next Saturday, I expect you will be there."

She looked embarrassed as she whispered, "I can't."

"Why?" I asked with a seductive pout, "You don't find me attractive?"

"No, I find you incredibly intoxicating. It is just," she paused for a long time, "I am only 20."

"Really? You look over 21," I said genuinely surprised.

Her face glowed with pride as she said, "Thanks, I turn 21 in a couple of months."

"Well," I said, "Do you want to see me again?"

"Desperately," she said eagerly.

"Well then meet at The Pheonix Club at 9:30 next Saturday. I know everyone there, if you come with me they will let you in."

"Really," she said like a little school girl, "I have wanted to go there forever."

"Well consider me your Fairy Godmother, but a lot younger, hotter and someone you want to fuck."

She laughed and said, "I will be there; what should I wear?"

"It is a high scale lesbian bar, so dress classy, yet sexy. Your outfit should showcase your assets and have the other woman drooling to please you, but should also be made so others can easily access your...," I paused for effect, "fun parts."

She said, "I have a few ideas."

"You understand," I cautioned, "That you are must obey all my commands when at the club."

She looked slightly surprised, but quickly regained her composure, "Well that goes without saying."

I smiled, "You are a little deviant, aren't you?"

She moved in, her hand on my ass, "In more ways than one." She moved to my ear and whispered, her hot breath on my neck, my weak spot by the way, "What about your friend?"

I responded, "She's straight, or at least she thinks she is."

As my hand slid under her skirt, just teasing her pussy through her panties, she moaned into my ear, "She's a dyke, even if she doesn't know it yet."

She nibbled my ear, my knees giving just a hair, giving away my weakness, as I responded, "That's my hope."

I kissed her again one more time and opened the door. I went to Mia and said, "Can I have my panties back?"

Mia sheepishly opened her purse and handed them to me.

I gave them to Sophia and said, "A gift for my little slave."

She smirked, looked around, slid off her panties and tossed them to me, "I can't take a gift without giving one back."

I grabbed them, handed her my phone and said, "Type in your number in case something comes up."

She grabbed the phone, expertly typed in her pertinent information and handed me back the phone.

I took it back, paid for my outfit, using her generous 25% discount, and Mia and I headed out. We headed over to Amanda's house for our once a month Bridge night where I purposely avoided Mia as much as possible, trying to play a little aloof. Although I did tell the girls about the new girl I met and how she would be a good little plaything for a while. The girls called me a lesbian slut and I shrugged my shoulders and agreed.

The school week went on with little fanfare as it was report card week, so both Mia and I were bombarded with work. Writing down comments for 48 kids in every category of learning is exhausting and brain-numbing. So on Friday, Mia and I went out for drinks, to celebrate another ending of report card reporting; Scott was out of town as was often the case. After a couple drinks we left, Mia saying she was exhausted and needed some sleep. I laughed and said it was only 7, but I too was pretty tired.

As we got in the car I said, "Can we make one more stop?"

Mia responded, "Sure, where else do you need to go?"

"The adult shop on 8th. I need a new toy or two for tomorrow night," I said rather matter-of-factly.

"Oh," Mia said surprised and seemingly a bit crestfallen.

"Plus, you being an old married hen pretty soon, we should get you some special toys for yourself. Scott is out of town a lot."

"I –I –I have a toy."

"I know, the same small, thin vibe you had in college isn't it?"

"Maybe," she said ever so slightly defiant.

"It is isn't it?" I said while laughing, "I was just kidding."

She responded all defensive, "I don't need it, Scott is all I need."

"Really, Scott is gone for weeks at a time, how do you survive? If I don't get off every day or two I am a complete mess."

"Every day or two?" Scott asked astonished.

"Usually every day, sometimes more than once, if I am being honest," I said honestly.

"Huh," Mia said contemplating, her mine seeming to go elsewhere.

"It's settled girlfriend, we are getting you some new play things." We drove in silence for the last couple minutes of the drive.

We entered the store and I went directly to the toys. Now I have a decent collection of adult accessories already, but I decided this was a great opportunity to up the ante on my seduction of my best friend.

The first thing I did was grab a pair of handcuffs. "Ever been handcuffed?"

Mia shook her head no.

"Well you really should try it. It is exhilarating when you are totally at the whim of someone else. It is, even better, to be the one handcuffing someone else. Suddenly you have all the power. These ones even glow in the dark, that would be pretty handy don't you think?" She didn't answer as I tossed a pair into a basket and said, "One can never have too many pairs." I then walked over to the vibrators. I grabbed a 7 inch black one and tossed it to Mia. "Is Scott this big?"

Mia blushed and looked at the toy as if it was an alien object.

"Twice as big as the one you have now." I then grabbed a 5 inch pink one with five speeds and said, "This may be more to your liking." I then took the black one and tossed it in the basket.

Mia looked at the toy as I moved to a double ended dildo, something I didn't actually have. I looked at them as a saleslady, a woman in her late 40s, black hair, clearly dyed, and hazel eyes, walked over. I asked her, "Any advice on what kind of double ended dildo one should buy?"

Mia dropped the toy when she realized someone else saw her with it.

The woman, clearly not fazed by such a question, answered, in a clearly British accent, "Well it depends on what you want. Our most popular, for women of experience, is our 7 inch long and a solid one inch thick double dong." She reached up to an upper shelf, where I got a good look at her still firm ass. She handed it to me still in its packaging.

"Have you ever used one yourself?" I asked teasingly.

She smiled and said, "Long ago in my college days."

"Was it effective?"

"Oh it did the trick."

Mia just watched the sexual verbal exchanges, not saying a word, yet seemingly hanging on every syllable.

I looked at it and burst out laughing. "Mia it's called the Pretty in Pink Double Dong. That is hilarious. Seriously, it even has two different John Hughes references."

Mia looked at me confused.

"Well the Pretty in Pink reference is obvious, but remember in 16 Candles that Chinese exchange student is named Dong," I explained. I then continued, "I have to get this." I placed it in the basket which was already half full.

The saleslady then handed me a much slimmer blue dildo called a Feeldoe Dildo. I looked at in awe. The saleslady explained, "This one is for a situation where one wants to be a little dominant and still get off at the same time."

"That sounds like me," I flirted.

"I thought it may," she said back.

"So how does it work?" I queried greatly intrigued.

"Well you see the one part goes inside you, while the other would go in your lover and you could actually use it as a penis to make love to her."

"Wow," I said, "Look MIa isn't this cool?"

Mia blushed again, but said, "It is creative."

"That it is," I said looking for a price. "Ouch," I said, "its 120 bucks."

The saleslady said, "It is expensive, but if you buy at least 5 toys, I will give you the special customer discount of 30 percent."

"Well in that case," I flirted, "How can I say no?" The saleslady put it in the basket for me.

"I also need a strap-on cock, preferably one that vibrates as well. Do they make such a thing?" I queried as Mia gave an awkward cough slash choke sound.

I looked at her and winked.

The British woman completely unfazed answered, "Yes they do. What length were you considering?"

"What length do you like?" I teased.

She chuckled as she said, "It has been many years since I have had the need for such a toy, but the women who come in here tend to like a couple different ones." She grabbed a black one that was eight inches long and said, "This one is for deep penetration, but I am told, by some very reliable sources, that women love it, especially if it is turned on high."

I grabbed the straps and wrapped it around my skirt. I asked, "Can you buckle it up for me?"

"Sure thing sweetheart" she responded and buckled me up. I was slightly disappointed that there was no sexual tension or teasing by her. Usually my flirting works on almost everyone. I decided I would have to turn on my charm.

I turned to Mia and said, "So how do I look?"

Mia stuttered and stammered questioningly, "Well, um, good?"

"Really, just good?" I teased feigning hurt feelings.

Mia quickly reiterated, "Well great for a girl with a strap-on, but isn't that way too big?"

"God no, I have had bigger cocks then this in me before. I won't even fuck anybody less than 7 inches now-a-days and that is only if I am desperate to get off." I paused, for dramatic effect, "Well that was the rule before I quit dating men and started fucking only women."

Mia looked bewildered and overwhelmed. I couldn't tell if she was turned on by me or repulsed.

The British saleslady broke the tension by upping the erotic tension when she said, "On the other hand, if you are into butt play, a smaller, thinner strap-on is better." She then handed me a pink cock.

I looked and said, "Good call, that eight inch would be too big for my ass, but this would fit snugly."

Mia stammered trying to get the words out, "You, you..."

I walked over to her and said astonished, "You have never had a cock in your ass? Ever?"

"God no," she said.

"Ever?" I said trying to press her buttons by acting like it was the most natural sexual act in the world.

"No, I would never do that," she said confidently.

I smiled and said, "Never say never, honey."

I dropped it in the basket and took off the one on my waist and dropped it in the basket also.

The saleswomen then said, "We do have a brand new product that I think you will really like."

"Do tell," I responded curiously.

She handed me a pink strap-on cock that had a second plug for the woman wearing the strap-on. I looked at it and said, "Does it vibrate?"

"Both do," she said and added, "The one could be in your vagina or butt while you pleasured your lover."

"Really," I said all excited.

"Yes, it is similar to the feeldoe, but this one vibrates and is cheaper."

I looked at the price; the vibrating duel harness, as it was called, was only 60 bucks. "Well, I think I will take this instead, um, what is your name?"

"Olivia," she said.

"Well Olivia, you have been amazingly helpful," I said as my hand gently caressed her arm.

"That is my job," she joked. "Now I get the feeling that you have a bit of a domination streak in you, am I correct?"

"Well," I shrugged nonchalantly.

"I have a very unique item if you are into extreme power trips in the bedroom."

"Do show?" I said.

She handed me a strange looking 6 inch long beige cock with a strap. I looked at her confused, "Another strap-on?"

She gave a soft sincere laugh as she said, "No, no, it's called the Accommodator. You wrap it around your lover's head and she can pleasure you with her face."

The light bulb went on as I said, "I can have my slut just fuck me with a cock on her face." Olivia shook her head yes and I said, "That is amazing." I looked at it closer and said, "I need to see it on someone."

I looked at Mia and decided to test the water just a bit and asked, "Mia will you audition it on for me."

"Um," she began awkwardly, but I just walked over and put it on her head.

"Wow, that is awesome," I said. "I'll take it." I quickly took it back off her so as to not humiliate her too long and tossed it into the full basket. I then noticed a hilarious named anal toy the Rump Shakers Vibrating Butt Plug which was 5 inches long, an inch wide and a crazy inch and a half at the base. I had never had anything that wide in my butt, but maybe someday. Plus it came with a remote control.

I asked, "How far can one control the butt plug?"

Oivia said, "I am not sure, let me check." She read the back of the box and after a minute or so said, "It doesn't say." With that, she opened the package and quickly inserted the batteries. She then handed me the plug. I turned it on. Olivia then used the remote to make it vibrate faster. With each speed she moved a few feet back.

"Wow", I said, "it works from at least 20 feet, that would be handy?"

Mia looked at me and said, "How?"

"Well say you have it in a girl's butt and want to get her off, you can do it from across the room."

Mia sarcastic, for the first time today, said, "Well obviously, who wouldn't need such a convenience." But I saw her head spinning as she contemplated all she saw today.

I tossed it in the basket, smiling right at Mia, and said, "Never know when this will come in handy. Olivia, which toy would be best for a girl who is always alone because her husband to be is always on the road?"

"Is she into kink?"

I looked at Mia, "Are you into kink?"

"God no," Mia said astonished by the question.

"No," I said to Olivia, who chuckled.

"Well then the we-vibe-2 is an amazing little toy that can be used by yourself, with a man or with a woman. It goes inside your vagina and the inside part vibrates hopefully hitting your g-spot while the outside vibrates on your clitoris." She handed on to me.

"Wow it is small and light," I said amazed for once myself.

"Yes, it is and you can have it inside you when you are being pleasured by a man's penis or one of your," pausing for effect, "special toys."

"Nice," I said. "Mia, your engagement present from me is this." I then tossed the small toy to her.

She caught it and looked at it closely. She turned it on and jumped a bit.

As she played with her toy, I whispered to Olivia, "I also need two jelly egg vibrators with remote."

She smiled, seemingly knowing my future purpose for them, as she said, "I will add them to your things."

"No, I am going to ask for one, but I need you to tell me that actually they are buy one, get one free. Of course, you can charge me for both."

"I understand," she said.

I leaned right into her ear, as I slipped her my card, "If you ever want to reminisce and relive your younger days with the toys give me a call."

She smiled, her face blushed, as she whispered back, "You never know sweetie, I just may take you up on that offer."

I nibbled on her ear briefly and said, "I would fuck you like no man ever has." I then moved away before she could respond and asked no longer whispering, "Olivia to you have any jelly eggs?"

"Yes actually, and they are on sale. Buy one, get one free and they come with a remote control similar to the one for your butt plug."

"Well Mia today is your lucky day; besides your little vibe thing there, you get a free jelly egg."

"What is a jelly egg?"

"It is a tiny little vibrating toy, shaped like an egg, that goes inside you and can tease and please you all day long," I explained handing her an egg and taking the vibe from her.

"Oh," she said, looking at the small egg.

"Thanks Mia, I think that is all I can afford today."

Olivia smiled and said, "Do you need any lube for the toys or anything?"

"No, no," I replied, "I've got lots of lube."

Olivia then took the basket and went to the till.

We followed and saw Olivia whisper something to her 18 year old employee. The young girl nodded her head in understanding.

I grabbed an anal starter's kit for 10 bucks on my way to the till; hopefully something I could use on Mia someday as well.

The brunette scanned all the items and then Olivia scanned her card and typed in 50%. I looked at her as she said, "You are now a gold card client." She handed me a business card with her name on it, Olivia Styles, and a cell phone number hand written, and continued, "You will always get 50% off anything you buy here. Call me anytime you need anything."

"Anything?" I asked, "That is a pretty broad word.

She flirted with me for the first time as she stressed, "Anything."

"Good to know and thank you very much, that is very sweet of you," I thankfully responded playing on the word sweetheart, she had earlier called me when she had no idea what was about to happen to her.

I grabbed the bag, pulled out Mia's we-vibe, and the medium sized vibrator I had forgot to take out when we picked the other vibe. I kept the extra egg for a later seduction.

I handed them to Mia, who sheepishly took them. Behind us we heard, "Mia, Claire, how are you?"

I turned around to see our principal, Amelia White, with her husband. Mia frantically pleaded to the teenager, "Please put these in a bag for me now."

The teenager obliged and handed Mia the bag. Amelia looked at my large bag and gave a smirk, but said nothing. We talked about nothing for a couple of minutes and then Mia and I headed out.

I burst out laughing as soon as we exited the building, "What do you think old bag Amelia would be doing in a sex shop?"

Mia just shrugged, still embarrassed from being seen in a sex shop.

"Probably buying a strap-on to fuck her husband with. I bet she wears the pants at home," I vulgarly suggested.

Mia just shook her head, used to my over-the-top commentary.

"Can you imagine, our principal wearing a strap-on...what a hoot," I exclaimed still laughing hard.

We got in the car and headed back home relatively in silence.

As I dropped Mia off I said, "Tell me how it works, I may have to get one of those myself."

Mia sighed slightly as she said, "I doubt I will try it tonight."

I said, with just a bit of a dominant tone, "Oh you are using it tonight. I want details. I didn't spend all that money for your new pleasure toy to sit in your nightstand."

"Um," she hesitated.

"No ums Mia," I said confidently, "Promise me you will use it tonight."

"Fine," she said, giving in like I thought she would, "I'll use it on myself."

"Good," I said, "I want to know if I should get myself one, now that I have a fifty percent discount."

Mia shook her head, "How do you always get so lucky?"

I smiled, "You can get lucky like that too. Mia, you just have to know how to talk the talk, flirt the flirt and flaunt the flaunt."

Mia began to get out of the car as I finished, "Tomorrow night, I am picking you up and we are going to The Pheonix Club."

Mia looked startled as she said, "The lesbian club?"

"Yep," I said matter-of-factly.

"I can't go there," she began.

"I have gone with you on double dates with complete losers; the least you can do is go with me once to my favourite club."

"Fine," she said, which meant it wasn't fine, but she would do it.

"What should I wear?"

"That red dress you wore at the Christmas party would work," I answered as I blew her a kiss and got out of there before she had a chance to change her mind.

I slept in past lunch, before slowly getting up for the day. I read the newspaper, called my mom, and finished the new Steve Martin novel "An Object of Beauty", which by the way is a riveting novel about the art world in America in the 1990s.

Around three, I called Mia. "Hi Darling," I cheerfully opened with.

"Hi," she responded, reluctance lingering in her tone.

"So, do you want to go out for supper and an early movie before heading to the club?"

"Sure," she said, after a slight pause, "Do we really have to go to The Pheonix though?"

"Yes," I said adamantly, "You have never been there and I think you should see and learn a bit of my lifestyle. I am a lesbian now and I don't see that changing."

"Sorry," she immediately said, "I didn't realize it was so important to you. Of course, we will go. But, I get to pick the movie."

"Fine," I said, feigning disappointment, "I was so hoping we would go and see Harry Potter part whatever it is."

"Funny," she laughed and said, "I was thinking that action movie with Angelina Jolie."

"OK, she's hot, I'd do her," I said continually pushing the envelope just a tad.

"She is hot, I might too," she surprised me back.

I laughed and said, "I'll pick you up at five."

I then went and decided what to wear for tonight. It took forever as I wanted to look powerful, seductive and sexy. I finally decided on the stockings I had bought at the shop from Sophia, a black dress that was sexy but classy, stopping just below the knee, but sexy enough to showcase my all my curves; matching black leather boots with a flashy three inch heel that went just below the knee. The dress, backless, did not allow for a bra, but I did have on a black thong.

I grabbed both the little eggs and a small vibe and dropped it in my purse, just in case. I did my make-up, and checked myself in the mirror; I looked pretty darn hot and headed over to pick up Mia.

I arrived early and knocked on her door. Scruffy, her adorable little poodle, yapped at the door until Mia opened it. She clearly did not want to look underdressed, as instead of the conservative, slightly sexy red dress I had suggested, she had on an amazing gold dress, a gown really, with matching four inch heels and beige pantyhose or stockings. Her hair was up and she had never looked this delicious. It really took all my will power not to just rape her right then. Instead I decided to flirt with her, "Wow, you look good enough to eat?"

"Olivia," she said all giddy, she had been drinking already, I concluded.

"No seriously," I said, "If you were not getting married in a couple of months, I would be all over you."

She blushed and I waited for what seemed like an eternity for her to respond, when she didn't, I finished, "But you are, so I guess I will have to devour someone else tonight." I looked at my watch and declared, "We should get going, we don't want to be late at McGiny's or they just give away your table."

We headed out and as I drove I noticed that her nails were done, something she seldom did. The rose red shined in contrast to the gold. "I see you did your nails gorgeous, what is the occasion?"

She looked at me and said with a surprisingly confident tone, "I figured if I was going to an upscale club, regardless of its clientele, I had to look upscale." She paused before blurting out "Plus, I want to know if I am lesbian hot."

"Lesbian hot?" I asked stunned.

"Yes," I know I am relatively attractive for the boys, but I have no idea if I can make a woman all excited."

"Are you going dyke on me?" I asked.

"Oh no," she said, "I would never cheat on Scott, but flirting is still fair game."

I purred, "And don't you worry, you are definitely lesbian hot."

She blushed as we arrived at the five star restaurant and I said, "Indeed, flirting is allowed, but be careful; some of the women at this club are very aggressive."

As we got out of the car she said, "Oh, I can take care of myself."

I smiled to myself, thinking seducing her may be easier than I thought, but said, "Oh I know you can,' but thinking that I was not so sure she could.

We went in to the restaurant and had a great meal as we talked about the wedding, which of course I hoped never would occur, but I played along like a maid of honour should. I asked questions, we discussed who to invite, blah, blah, blah. The whole time I just kept thinking how badly I wanted to make love to her; to declare my love for her.

As we ate I said, finally changing the depressing topic, "So you know the waiter has been checking you out all night."

"I thought he was giving my chest area a little more attention," she responded somewhat confidently.

"Want to freak him out completely?" I asked.

"How?" she inquired.

"Pretend to be a lesbian," I devilishly put forward.

"How would I do that?" she asked considering the idea.

At that moment the waiter came to the table and asked, "So how is everything tonight?" His eyes, moved slightly lower to check out Mia's cleavage.

"Oh good," I said, "The food is excellent."

Mia, now suddenly shy, said, "Yes, it is very delicious."

I got up then and decided to take a small risk and moved to Mia and leaned in and gave her a three second tender kiss. I then stood back up and said, "I am going to the ladies room lover, be right back."

The look on both Mia's and the waiter's eyes was one of complete shock. Mia's look was one of bewildered surprise, while the waiter's was more of a 'wow, did I just see what I thought I saw' look.

When I returned, Mia was on a second glass of wine. I sat down and said, "Sorry if that was awkward, but the look on his face was way worth it, don't you think?"

Mia responded too quickly, "Oh yeah, that was hilarious." I could tell that she was still trying to process what had occurred. But in my mind it was clear, she enjoyed it.

Our waiter checked back on us every couple of minutes, each time lingering a couple seconds longer than necessary.

When he gave us the bill I saw that his phone number was on it. I smirked. I looked at the waiter and said, "Neither of us swing that way, but do you like to watch?"

The guy, who probably seemed confident when he put his number down, now was way out of his league. He babbled, "Um, yeah, I."

Mia, surprising me, stood up, moved towards him, and whispered just loud enough for him and me to hear, "Ever seen two women fuck?"

I coughed, almost choking on the mint I had just popped in my mouth; but I recovered quickly as I added, "Maybe we could add a real cock, honey?"

Mia playing along said, "Yeah, think you could handle us both?"

The guy was as red as an apple and he barely was able to answer, "Yeah, I, could."

Finally I broke the awkward situation by saying, "Well, we got your number." I kissed his cheek and Mia and I left laughing so hard tears came down her face.

As we drove to the movie I said, "You know, you played lesbian pretty well, girlfriend."

She retorted, "Well I have watched you seduce quite a few women the last couple years."

"Are you calling me a slut?" I asked acting all sarcastically insulted.

"No, no," she said all apologetic, not catching my sarcasm, "It's just watching your seductions have always been rather entertaining."

"Really?" I asked, "I thought that repulsed you. I have often been tamer than I usually am."

"I am not repulsed by it. I accept you for who you are and if you are interested in women, then so be it. Actually," she continued, "watching you play the seduction game with girls has been fun to watch and kind of hot."

I decided not to pursue this now as we didn't have enough time to discuss this the way I wanted to. So I said with a purr, as the movie theatre came into view, "Well, I will try to really entertain you tonight."

Mia did not respond and I could not read her face. Either she was jealous of my relations with other women or she was just a supportive friend. Which was it? Or maybe it was both. I decided right then as I parked the car that tonight I would try to make her jealous. Try to get her to play all her cards. If I played mine correctly, I may be able to play her bluff. But first I had to raise the stakes.

At the movie we split up as I got the tickets and she got the popcorn. It was our usual routine, almost like an old married couple I reflected.

By the time we got to our seats the previews, all seven of them (why are there so many fucking previews), were under way. We watched the movie in silence, sharing popcorn and Swedish berries. I made sure to time my popcorn reaches for when she did, so we would often brush hands, both of us lingering in the popcorn container longer than we ever had as I pretended to reach for popcorn. I really felt like a teenager in high school when a boy would take me to a movie and he would make slight moves to see how far he could get. I wanted to push it further, but I didn't.

The movie ended, it was like all Angelina Jolie movies, not bad, but not as good as it could have been. The movie was longer than expected and we headed to the club at 9:35, already five minutes late. We drove talking about the movie and its relative lameness as we headed to the club and I embarked on the next step of the seduction plan.

By the time we arrived at the club I was worried about a couple of things and I never worried. I was usually confident and sure of myself, but this uncertainty of how Mia felt for me was overwhelming me with self doubt, I certainly didn't want to harm our friendship. My first worry was how Mia would react to the club and its surroundings, although I felt she would be fine; my second worry was would Sophia still be there when I was already twenty-five minutes late? That said, I would eventually learn that both worries were nothing more than that.

As we got to the club entrance I saw Sophia, waiting, in a classic red dress, with black nylons, and matching red three inch pumps. As soon as she saw me she smiled, but when she saw Mia the smile disappeared. I said, "So sorry I'm late, the movie was longer than we thought it would be and traffic was brutal."

She put on her fake smile and said, "No worries. I was late myself."

I ignored that, I didn't like disobedience, (I told her 9:30) but she was in an awkward situation. She clearly usually was the seductress and not the prey. She was trying to play the game, but truthfully she did not know how to play it from this perspective.

As we entered, not carded of course, I asked the security guard, "What time did my young slut in the red arrive?"

He answered with a sly smile, "About 9:15."

"Thanks stud," I said and gave him a kiss on the cheek.

I smiled to myself, she had not disobeyed, and actually she was eagerly early.

We walked into the heart of the club and found the last unoccupied table. We sat down and ordered our drinks. It was still a bit early, the place usually didn't get crazy until11, but some action was already under way. I said nothing as both the young dyke and my hopefully future dyke became immersed in the sexuality of the scene. The dance floor was only about a third full, but entertainment was still available.

While most of the women were dancing as though it was any other club, a couple of couples were not. Two women were kissing passionately, each with the other's ass in their hands, while in the corner, a woman, at least 40, had her dressed raised and a girl, probably in her mid-twenties, had her hand under the dress and was clearly fingering her.

When Mia saw this she had a look of complete surprise, yet she did not look away. Sophia was looking everywhere trying to take it all in.

I said to Mia, "It is rude to stare."

Mia looked away and to me and said, "I just can't believe anyone would do something so intimate in such a public place."

I smiled and said, "Oh that is nothing. In here everything goes. See over there, the woman in the gold cocktail dress. That is Megan, she is a friend of mine. Look closer, can you see the shoes from under the table?" (Author's note: If you want to learn more about Megan and her seduction of her 18 year old babysitter read my Bedding the Babysitter series...the last half of part 2 occurs at the exact same time as this chapter.)

Mia did and it took her a while to process what was clearly occurring. "Is she?"

Sophia answered for me as she said, "She is being serviced, isn't she?"

"Yes, she is. And you see that younger girl who just returned to the table?"

"Yes," Sophia said.

"This is her first time here."

"How do you know," Sophia inquired.

"Look at her. She is constantly looking around, but not making eye contact. She keeps fidgeting with her hands. Her face clearly displays both nervousness and insecurity. I bet she has only come out in the past month, maybe even the past week. Actually knowing Megan, that young ripe girl just lost her lesbian cherry last night."

"Wow," said Sophia star struck.

All three of us watched as two other girls joined Megan at the table and then saw the girl crawl back up from underneath. After a minute or two, a second girl crawled under the table. Finally, Mia shot her second drink since getting here as she said, "Really?"

I turned to her and said, "Everyone feels safe here. You can let out any sexual inhibitions and what happens at the club, stays at the club. For example, watching all this has made me pretty horny and I have a cute little dyke craving my pussy don't I?"

Mia briefly thinking I was referring to her began to protest, weakly I may add, "I, um, am getting married."

But she caught on when I said, "Sophia, on your knees."

Sophia looked at Mia, smiled and said, "If she won't please you, I will." She got on her knees and crawled under the table. I opened my legs, making sure my knee touched Mia's. I felt my thong move slightly and then a tongue began lightly lapping my already very wet pussy.

As Sophia tenderly licked my cunt, I explained to Mia, who was well on her way to being drunk, "Mia, I love the power of submission. For example, the little dyke under the table right now, is not someone I will love, but she is someone to have fun with. If I told her to, she would lick your cunt after she got me off. She will do everything I say tonight." I paused and moaned when Sophia slid a finger inside me, before continuing, I looked Mia right in the eye, hinting at my true feelings, and said, "That said, I want to fall in love. Unconditional, honest, heart-stopping love. I want to share everything I am with the one I love."

Mia responded sincerely, "Oh honey, you will find that love." Her hand rested on my leg.

I looked her straight in the eye and responded, "I already found it; she just doesn't know it yet."

Mia contemplated this, I think unaware at my implication, and said, "Well you have to tell her, show her, love is worth the risk."

I reflected on this said, "You think so?"

"I know so," she said, "No one would resist your charm."

"You did?" I teased, my moaning getting louder, "Hmmm, yes, I'm cumming, don't stop slut." I squeezed my legs around my little dyke's head as my orgasm sent shivers throughout my whole body.

As Sophia returned to the table, I realized this was a perfect chance to seduce Mia. I may never get a better chance, but she was drunk and I wanted our love, if it was to happen, to be built on a stronger platform. So I changed the subject as I said to Sophia, "You are a damn fine pussy pleaser."

She blushed slightly and said, "I aim to please."

Showing my dominance to Mia, who seemed annoyed that Sophia now had my attention, I asked, "So Sophia, if I asked you to crawl back under this table and please Mia here, would you?"

"Of course," she said obviously, "I would turn this straight girl into a dyke overnight."

I laughed; Mia blushed and looked around, avoiding eye contact of either of us.

I asked, "Mia, do you need to get off?"

Mia shook her head no, still not looking at us.

Sophia shrugged, "Her loss."

I then said, "Indeed it is. So Sophia, you are free to go mingle."

Mia and I sat in silence as Sophia disappeared into the growing crowd and I just kept bringing up seductive talks to get Mia turned on.

"Oh yeah, just talking about it makes me want to do again, plus the dirty submission gets me off." I said

"I can't imagine." Mia replied

"Really?" I asked, "I am guessing that when you and Scott are in bed, he is the one in control. Isn't he?"

Mia looked down and after a long, long pause said, "I suppose."

"Girlfriend, you can tell me," I said supportively, "After all, you know everything about me now."

Mia paused and then said, "Yes, Scott is the aggressor in the bedroom."

"Do you obey him?" I questioned.

"Yes, I suppose I do."

"And it gets you off being submissive to him?"

"Yes," she blushed.

"So you and I are not much different then. Only I like to be in charge usually. I like to make a woman go places she only dreamed about. I like to get them to take risks that are extreme. With such submission, comes complete pleasure."

Mia was hypnotized by my words. I knew I could take her now, but I wanted to wait; they say all good things come to those who wait. Plus I didn't want to just fuck her, which would be easy; I wanted her to fall in love with me. I wanted her to completely submit to me as a lover. So I said, "Time for a dare."

Mia looked at me questioningly as I opened my purse and pulled out the two eggs. I turned them on and inserted one in my pussy. I then handed the other to her and said, "I dare you to put this egg in you until we leave the club."

Mia took the egg, looked at it, and without saying a word, without breaking eye contact, inserted the egg inside her pussy. I smiled and said, "Let's dance."

I grabbed her hand and led her to the dance floor. As we danced it was clear she was drunker than I thought. Twice she stumbled forward and I caught her from falling. I took the first opportunity to slide my hand up the back of her ass, my hand staying way longer than necessary. The second time I actually caught her by her breasts, and leaned her back up, my hands still cupping her large breasts.

When the song ended, she said she had to pee so I took her to the bathroom. As she came out of the bathroom I noticed that her face looked like she had been drifting illusions as she was in the bathroom and then I went on to ask, "You saw yourself between a female's legs didn't you?"

Mia shook her head yes as she whispered in the quietest voice ever, "Yes."

I encouraged her, "It is ok, it is natural."

"But I am not gay. I am getting married this summer."

I gave her a friendly supportive hug as I said, "It's ok. Finding a woman attractive, or being turned on by a woman, does not make you gay. But if you don't do it now, you will always wonder what if."

"You think so," she said falling in my web.

"I know so. I had to try cock to know I was a lesbian; you need to try pussy to know you love men."

My bizarre logic seemed to work for her as she said, "That makes sense." So I decided to take her to this stall at a side of the club where there was this lady we called Rosie and everyone would want to please her as she has a very cute vagina and she was really pretty. We usually lined up to get her pleased.

Big Rosie's trademark orgasm exploded from the stall and a very cute pregnant woman exited the stall.

I said, "Mia here is your chance. You can go before me."

Mia looked at me with extreme trepidation as Rosie bellowed, "Get your ass in here dyke."

Mia quickly turned and entered the stall. I then heard Rosie say, "You are new. What is your name?"

"Mia."

"And why are you here now?"

Mia paused and said, "To, um, eat your vagina."

Rosie's laugh bellowed as she said, "Eat my vagina? That's a new one." There was a pause, "Hey you are the one who was watching earlier weren't you?"

"Yes," Mia answered embarrassed.

"You are quite shy; I don't get too many shy ones waiting to dive into my pussy. What is your story?"

"Um, I don't know. I have never done this before, but when I watched the black woman between your legs I was mesmerized and although my mind said to look away, my body had different ideas." Mia tried to explain.

"So this is your first time eating pussy?"

"Yes," she answered.

"I love virgins," Big Rosie said.

Megan looked back to the stall and said "And it has been relatively quiet ever since."

As Megan finished the story I questioned "How long as she been in there?"

"About 10 minutes," I would guess.

"I just can't believe it," I said, shaking my head dumfounded. We sat there in silence until I heard Big Rosie, "That's it my straight little pussy eater. Keep licking right there." Rosie's moans got louder and then Mia brought Rosie to an orgasm. I waited as Mia stood up and I heard Rosie say, "Who brought you here?"

"My friend Claire," Mia answered.

Rosie said very accurately, "You know she brought you here with an ulterior motive?"

"No," Mia said, "we have been best friends since high school; she is my maid of honour."

"And she wants to have you between her legs, I guarantee it," Rosie assured her.

"I don't think so," Mia said with less conviction.

"Trust me, I know Olivia. You will be between her legs very soon. That I promise," Rosie confidently predicted.

I then said to Megan, "I don't want her to know I know what she has been doing, so tell her that I will be back at my table."

"Sure thing," Megan replied and I walked out of there and returned to my table. I looked at my watch; it was almost midnight. Sophia would be gone by now. My pussy was so wet from seeing Mia's submission. I knew now I could have her, but how would I know if she loved me. I wanted it all; her submission and her love. Could I have both?

I looked around hoping to see someone I could pull under the table to have a quick orgasm, but didn't see anyone I knew. I then saw Candace Carter, the TV celebrity, who never said no to a pussy and called her over. "Hi, Candace," I said.

"Hi, Claire," she responded, "You look amazing as usual."

"Thanks," I said and then asked, "Are you hungry?"

She smiled and said, "Famished," and crawled under the table. She began licking, using her lips as well, in a way few others did. I continued to scan the crowd looking for Mia, who finally returned from her bathroom marathon. As she walked back to the table I noticed her face was shiny, clearly still covered from Rosie's cum, walking my way.

She sat down and said, "I thought you left without me."

"I would never do that," I said sincerely.

Mia looked at me and said, "It's ok. I found a way to make the time pass." She paused, trying to find the right way to tell me, "I never left the bathroom. Some older woman took me into a stall and ate my pussy and then I," she paused, trying to get the words out.

I helped break her awkward struggle by saying, "You ate out Rosie."

Her face red as can be said, "Yes."

"It's ok Mia," I said, my hand on her leg, "She is almost irresistible. It doesn't make you a lesbian."

"But," she said, "I loved it."

"Oh," I said.

"I promised Big Rosie I would return in two weeks."

"Really?" I asked.

"Yes," she confirmed, she moved in toward me, I think to kiss me, until she noticed that someone was under the table. She suddenly went stiff and said icily, "Someone is under the table again, isn't there."

"Yes," I said, now frustrated that I had clearly disappointed her. I tried to explain, "I went looking for you and talked to Megan and anyways I can't explain it, I got all horny again and well," I paused, "Candace Carter is under the table."

Mia's icy look broke a bit as she said, "Carter really?"

"In the flesh," I said as I tried not to let a moan escape. But Candace was an expert between a woman's legs; plus the egg vibrating inside me and Mia's submission was too much and I screamed a variety of odd sounds as my body exploded with joy.

Mia watched the whole time and I was surprised when she lifted the table skirt and demanded, "Slut, do me now."

My mouth dropped and Mia smiled and said, "How often am I going to get a chance to have a celebrity get me off. Plus this fucking egg is driving me nuts."

We sat in silence as Candace pleased Mia and triggered an orgasm in her in only a couple of minutes. Candace then crawled out from under the table, cum still on her lips, and said, "Let's see the face of the cunt I just ate." She smiled and said, "Hi, I'm Candace."

Mia smiled and said, "I know who you are, I am Mia."

"It is very, very nice to meet you," Candace said, "Your pussy was delicious."

Mia smiled and said looking directly at me, "That is good to know."

I realized that I was no longer the seductress, but had become the prey. That said, Mia was still drunk, not 'I am going to be sick' drunk, but rather, 'I only did what I did because I was drunk' drunk.

We talked about our jobs and politics for a bit until Candace said, "Well, I have my eye on one more tasty treat tonight." She stood up, "It was a pleasure."

"Yes it was," Mia and I responded in unison; we then broke out laughing as Candace left.

"So," I said, "We should get you home, you are kind of drunk."

She shrugged and said, "I suppose." She then shot her last drink. I finished mine and we headed out.

We stopped to watch a woman in her 70s getting fisted by a girl who couldn't be more than 20. Mia starred too. The grandma screamed as the hand disappeared inside her gaping hole as the younger girl called her grandma slut. We also saw the same pregnant woman fucking herself with the end of a beer bottle as she watched the fisting. I shook my head and grabbed Mia's hand as we exited the club. I held her hand all the way to the car and helped her get in. The night clearly had overwhelmed Mia and all her energy had been drained from her. We drove home in silence and I actually had to wake her up when we got her house. To both our surprise, her husband's car was in the driveway.

Mia suddenly sobered up in a millisecond as she said, "Oh my God, I still have pussy all over my face." She looked in her purse frantically looking for something to wipe her face clean. She did the best she could, but then she realized what she was wearing. "How am I going to explain this outfit?' she fretted.

I said, "Calm down. Phantom of the Opera is in town. Tell him you and I got all dolled up for a nice supper and a show. Technically that is all true. We did go out for a supper and we definitely saw a show. He will assume it is the play you saw."

This seemed to relax her a bit. I then added, "You should probably take that toy out."

"Oh yeah," she said, "I was beginning to get use to its slight teasing." She awkwardly took out the toy and put it in her purse. She got ready to leave and said, "Well that was very educational."

"That it was," I agreed. I then said to ease her conscience, "Whatever happens at the club, stays at the club."

She shook her head in agreement and said, "Well thanks, that was fun."

"I am happy you enjoyed yourself," I said slyly back. I leaned in as if I was going to kiss her lips and watched as she closed her eyes waiting for the kiss. Instead my lips just brushed hers ever so lightly before I gave her a kiss on the cheek.

A sigh escaped her lips, but she smiled as if she wasn't disappointed, even though she was. "Good night," she finally said.

"Good night," I returned and watched her leave. I followed her with my eyes the whole way in as I anticipated the look back. It didn't come as early as I expected, but it came, as she reached the door. She looked back at me and smiled. I blew her a kiss and drove home.

The drive home was a blur as I reflected on the night. I now had confirmation she was submissive and I now knew she was willing. The only question left was did she love me. Would she cancel the wedding and declare her love for me? I still didn't know, but I was hopeful. I smiled as I thought that the final part of my plan would begin on Monday; a two week long onslaught of affection which would hopefully cumulate in a declaration of love to her and hopefully a similar declaration from her to me.

I purposely did not call her on Sunday. I wanted to let the night just linger inside as she sobered up and dealt with her fiancé. I spent the day doing laundry, planning lessons and watched a movie. I love how people think if you're a lesbian all you ever do is think sex. I was a complete person with a variety of passions and only Mia really knew the complete me.

On Monday we met at school and acted as if nothing had happened only two days earlier. I asked how Scott was and she said, "Same old, same old."

"Is that a good or bad thing?" I asked trying to delve deeper for a secret meaning.

"Not good," she said, "He was home for the first time in five days and all we wanted to do was watch hockey." She paused and then stressed "Hockey."

"Well you know men, they have very limited interests. Sex, food and sports."

"Well he only seems to have two," she said frustrated.

Later, at the end of day she came in to my room all flushed and said, "I got flowers sent to me." She looked at me all freaked out, "At work."

I had sent the flowers so playing dumb I said, "Well that is romantic. At least he is trying."

"They are not from him," she said perturbed and handed me a card.

Lovely Mia,

You are a beautiful woman. You deserve only the best.

Lovingly,

A secret admirer...

P.S.-That gold dress looked amazing on you.

"Oh," I said, "Who could it be from?"

"I don't know," she said, "Could it be someone from the club?"

"Who?" I asked.

"I don't know," she said.

"I wouldn't worry about it. Just enjoy them," I recommended. "Actually, you should take them home and show them to Scott."

"I can't do that," she said.

"I suppose not," I said. I looked at the clock and said, "Got to go coach volleyball."

Mia looked at me all concerned, "Are you going to be ok?"

"I'll be fine. Everyone knows the rules. What happens at the club..."

"Stays at the club," Mia finished.

I kissed her on the cheek and headed out.

On Tuesday I didn't see Mia till after school as it was a hectic day. I walked into her classroom and said, "Those really are nice flowers."

Mia gave a slight grin and said, 'The nicest I have ever got."

"That is too bad," I said, "A girl needs simple symbols of love on a regular basis. We need to feel loved."

"I don't feel too loved right now," she said with a frown.

"What's wrong? What did he do?"

"He won't be home for Valentine's Day. He will be in Toronto. He won't even be in the same country. Some special conference."

"Fuck off," I said, "That bastard. He knows how much you love Valentine's Day."

"He said he had no control over it. He said, we can celebrate this weekend," she said with tears in her eyes.

I opened my purse, grabbed my phone and called Susan. "Hi Susan. Do you have any openings today? Five o'clock. Great. No, it's for my friend Mia. Yes, give her the full treatment." I hung up and said "I got you an appointment for a full body massage."

She looked at me confused.

"You are all stressed. Go see Susan. She gives the most amazing massages in the world," I advised.

She said, "Well I could certainly use one." I gave her a card with the address on it. She took it and said, "What would I do without you?"

I laughed and said, "Probably wither away and die."

Mia laughed as I headed out.

Thursday came and I returned to work and it was like Groundhog Day, except in reverse. This time Mia was out with the flu. I coached volleyball again and ended up going out for drinks with half the team. Again, no great story, other than I had a couple too many drinks and ended up sick for a second straight day, although this one was self-inflicted.

The final part of my plan fell into place on Friday. As the day ended, I went into Mia's room and said, "I have a plan."

Mia looked at me skeptical as she said, "You do, do you."

"Yes, is your man still gone on Valentine's Day?"

"Yes," she said, "Thanks for reminding me."

"Well, I decided we will make it a special girl's night in."

"Really," she said, "You have no plans?"

"Yes, I do," I said, "with my best friend."

Mia lit up as she said, "That would be awesome."

"We'll make exact plans later, but let's plan to just leave from here and no matter what we do, we will end up at my place. Bring jammies, we are having a two person slumber party."

"Wow, that is so high school," she reflected, "I love it."

I then gave her my now traditional kiss on the cheek and headed out. I was going back home for the weekend to visit the parents. Mia was supposed to be having her early Valentine's Day celebration with her man. I got in my car and headed the four hours it would take to get home, beginning my final countdown to the seduction of my best friend.

The weekend was fun but now it was Monday and it was time to start the final stage of my lesbian seduction I had a courier drop off a box just as school ended. The box included a card and a gift. The card read:

Sexy Mia,

Still thinking about you.

Your secret lesbian admirer.

P.S. The gown is for you for Saturday. I look forward to seeing you again at The Pheonix Club.

The gown was a slinky halter gown that was completely backless and had a front v-neck opening that went to the belly button. Obviously it could not be worn with a bra. The outfit would be perfect for the annual day after Valentine's party at The Pheonix Club. A legendary annual party that I hoped to take Mia to as my date.

I walked into her room after school as she was looking at the gown. I said, "Wow, that is an amazing dress. Where did you get it?"

She handed me a card and I read it. "Oooh, the secret admirer strikes again."

Mia looked at it more and said, "Well my secret admirer treats me way better then my fiancé."

"Are you still going on Saturday?"

"I don't know," she responded reflectively.

"The fact that you didn't say no, means you probably will."

She looked at me and said, "I can't explain it, but I feel like I have to go back. It is almost all I think about."

"Oh, I understand it," I said adding, "completely."

She smiled and said, "I suppose you do. Do you think the secret admirer is Rosie?"

"I doubt it, it is not her style," I said honestly.

"Then who?" she pondered.

"I have no idea," I lied.

I gave her a hug and kiss on the cheek and headed out to coach.

On Tuesday that morning, before school started, Mia came in my room to borrow crayons and I said, "Hey I forgot all about it, but how was that we-vibe thing."

She responded, "Amazing actually. The way it hits and vibrates on both the g-spot and the clit is exhilarating."

"So I should get one," I said.

"Oh definitely, although with all your toys it may be just another one."

I responded, "Are you jealous of my toy collection?"

"No," she said, "I'm jealous of your sex life."

The first bell rang just as the conversation was getting interesting. Mia went to class and I prepared for mine.

At lunch a box of chocolates was delivered to Mia, by me secretly of course, with another note.

Elegant Mia,

For your sweet-spot, until I can taste your sweet-spot.

Your secret and hopeful lover

Mia came into my room at last break and said, "I got another gift."

I smiled and said, "She is really pulling out all the stops."

"It is driving me nuts not knowing," she said.

"You really like this attention, don't you?"

She shrugged, "It is nice to be noticed again."

"Slut," I said mockingly.

Mia looked at me and said sarcastically, "Are we really going to play that game?"

I feign confusion, "What could you possibly mean?"

"You do a different girl every day," she accused.

I went for the kill when I said, "Actually you have more recently ate pussy than I have."

Mia looked at me surprised and said, "Really?"

"Yep," I said, "I am in quite a drought. My cunt may shrivel up and die."

This made Mia burst out laughing as she left to get back to her class before recess ended.

The following day when I woke up and checked my phone I saw a distraught message from Mia.

February 12th 12:17AM

From: Mia

Claire,

I tried calling you, but you must be in bed already. I really need to talk to you, Scott and I had a huge fight.

Mia

That morning I called her and didn't get an answer. So I got to school early and as expected she was already there. I walked into her room, with two coffees, and asked, "So what is the story?"

She broke down crying instantly and through sniffles and so forth I got out of it that she confronted him about his lack of attention of late and that led to a shouting match and he walked out.

I got her calmed down and asked, "Does he make you happy?"

"Two weeks ago I would have said yes, but now I don't know," she answered honestly.

"Well maybe you guys need a break. If you are meant to be, it will all work out."

"I suppose" she said.

The rest of the day was crazy and I sent more flowers to her. I got the message changed at the last minute.

Glorious Mia

I can't stop thinking about you.

Your sexy smile;

Your luscious legs;

You are perfection to me.

Your secret admirer

P.S.-You deserve someone who will make you the only star in their universe.

After school Mia was jubilant and there was little evidence of her earlier emotional breakdown. That night we went out to a high school play version of Shakespeare's Othello. It was a simple night of friendship.

Thursday February 13th

I barely got to see Mia today as I took my students' on a field trip. I did make sure to send her another note and present. The note was only a few words:

Sweet Mia,

I long to kiss you,

To touch you,

To make love to you.

Your secret admirer

The present was a bottle of perfume.

Friday February 14th

That day, I sent no note.

When I saw her at school, I was happy to notice she was wearing the perfume I had bought her yesterday. I looked at her in her conservative black skirt and simple white blouse and my cunt got wet.

I said, "Happy Valentine's Day, gorgeous."

"You too," she replied.

I handed her a Mickey Mouse Valentine's Card that said, "I heart you." I signed it saying 'I hope all your romantic dreams come true.'

She read it and gave me a big hug.

We made final plans for our special girl's night and went about our day.

The day ended and Mia said as we drove to her place to pick up her travel bag, "I got no letter today."

"Oh," I said, "That is strange."

"Yeah," she said, "I was getting used to it."

"I know," I said, "It seemed to really boost your spirits."

"It did," she agreed, "Now that Scott is gone, it was a great validation." She paused, "Plus, I really want to know who the hell it is."

"Gone to Toronto or gone, gone?" I asked.

"Oh, I think gone, gone; I do deserve someone better," she said confidently.

"Yes, you do," I agreed.

We arrived at her house and I waited in the car. She took longer than I expected, but when she did return she had changed. She was wearing a flattering blue mini dress with mocha pantyhose, the dress to short for stockings.

I said, "Holy shit, now we have to go to my place so I can change."

We drove to my place and I took in her bag. I looked in my closet and choose a white mini dress with a very flattering neckline. I put on a pair of white pantyhose as well. I headed back to the car.

Mia said, "Wow, you look amazing in white."

"Thanks. I have never worn this before."

We drove to Rizzo's, a restaurant that was having a special four course meal for Valentine's Day. We went in and got strange looks as the only pair that were not man and woman.

We sat at a table, in a secluded corner, and were greeted by a very pretty blonde waitress. Her blue eyes just drew you in. She was dressed in the standard restaurant black skirt, black pantyhose and white blouse.

"Good evening, my name is Kate and I will be your server tonight."

Mia, surprising me, flirted, in a seductive voice, "What will you be serving?"

A bit of water sprayed out of my mouth as I heard Mia ask such a double entendre. Kate blushed but continued, "What can I get you to drink?"

"Some of your special juice," Mia asked.

Kate went even redder as I said, "Two glasses of red wine." As Kate went away to grab our drinks I asked, "What has gotten into you?"

She shrugged and said, "I don't know. Watching you flirt with other woman has always been a bit of a turn on; I thought I would do it myself."

"I usually know if she is a lesbian or bi-curious before I turn on the charm," I said.

"She's a dyke," Mia said confidently.

"How do you know? I have not even figured it out yet," I asked.

"Well it could be the way she looked at us; the way she took a peak at your legs as she reached our table; or it could be the way her eyes took quick glances at my cleavage as she spoke," she said like an expert seductress.

I laughed, "Interesting. I thought maybe you were going all lesbian on me."

She looked me in the eye and said, "Maybe I am going all lesbian on you."

As I considered her statement, Kate returned with our wine. I watched and indeed she did check out Mia's breasts. She then said, "Your first course will arrive shortly."

I watched her walk away and when I looked at Mia she was smirking at me as she said, "Told you."

We talked about school for a couple minutes until our bruschetta arrived. I asked Kate, "Have I seen you somewhere before?"

Kate looked at me and said, "I don't think so?"

"You look really familiar," I said.

"I get that a lot," she responded and then left to go to another table.

Mia said, "How dare you? She was my seduction."

I smiled and said, "Is it dare time?"

"Yes it is, but I suggest a double dare," she said deviously.

"Do tell," I asked intrigued.

"First," she began, "We both flirt with her and see who can get her number."

"OK," I said, "Easy enough."

"Second," she continued as she reached for her purse, "We both put these in our cunts for the rest of the night." She then handed me a jelly egg.

My face went red, which never happens, as I took the egg; plus Mia is not one for using such a vulgar world as cunt. Mia took a bite of her bruschetta as she smirked at me. I was completely out of my element; was she seducing me?

I get up to go to the washroom when Mia stopped me and commanded, "No, no, no, put it inside you here."

I looked at her, smiled and said, "Really, what has gotten into you?"

"Nothing yet," she teased back.

I turned it on low, looked around and awkwardly inserted the egg into my pussy which was rather difficult because I was wearing pantyhose and not stockings like I usually did.

Mia smiled as she took another bite of her bruschetta.

I asked, "Are you not putting yours in?"

"All in good time," she answered and ate more of her bruschcetta and put the egg on the table in the open for anyone to see.

Frustrated I began my appetizer. After we finished our bruschcetta in silence, Kate came back to grab the plates.

Kate saw the egg, looked slightly confused as Mia looked at her and said, "It's a toy. Have you ever used one?"

Kate shook her head no as Mia continued, "You should it feels amazing." Mia then took the egg, turned it on so the soft vibration sound could be heard, while starring at Kate, and put it inside herself. She then gave a soft moan. "Kate you have got to try this."

Kate stood memorized in trance as I said, "Kate, could I get a second glass of wine?"

Kate looked at me and said, "Yes ma'am," and she walked away.

I said, "Mia, this is a new you."

"You are to blame," she countered.

"How so?" I asked.

"I have been jealous of your lifestyle forever. You always are so happy."

"You seemed happy," I said concerned.

"I have not been for a long time," she said solemnly.

"You know, I am most happy when I am hanging out with you," I admitted.

"You are?"

"Of course. I love teaching, I love spending time with my family and I love hanging out with you. My sex life is just another part of who I am. I enjoy it, but it only brings temporary joy."

"Oh," she said reflectively.

Kate returned with our salads and we ate them in silence. As we finished our salads, Mia finally asked, "Can I ask you a question?"

"Anything?" I answered.

"Why have you never hit on me? Do you not find me attractive?" she asked insecurely.

I let out a gasp I was so surprised by the question. "Um, first off I find you the most beautiful person I know both inside and out. But I would never do anything that would ruin our friendship. You seemed so in love with Scott that I just never thought you would be into me in that way."

Mia looked at me as she took in my response. A guy, probably 20, came and took our plates and Kate followed behind with our main course. Kate asked, "Is there anything else I can get you ladies?"

"Your phone number," I asked.

Kate blushed again as Mia said, "Or you could just meet us at The Pheonix Club tomorrow night at 9:30."

I then said, "And please just bring us a bottle of whatever wine this is."

Kate said, "Yes ma'am" and left.

Mia asked "Is our seduction working?"

"I think so, but it is hard to tell. She can't give away too much while working," I responded.

"I suppose so," she reflected, "So you do find me attractive?"

I smiled and said, "Mia who do you think has sent you all those notes and cards the past two weeks?"

The lightbulb went on as she gasped, "It was you?"

"Yes Mia. I love you. I love you as a friend. But I also love you completely."

She looked at me taking it all in, "You mean."

"Yes, I want to spend the rest of my life with you. I want to hold your hand in public. I want to go to bed every night with you. I want to make love to every part of you."

"I love you too," she responded. "I just never thought, I mean, I just."

I stood up, moved to her side of the table, sat down and then leaned in for a kiss. It was as gentle as a kiss can be. She kissed back and soon our tongues were exploring each other's mouths. I broke the kiss when I heard a sound. I turned around and said, "Oh, more wine." I stood up and returned to my side.

Kate looked at us in a stunned state. She slowly recovered and said, "Can I get you anything else?"

I smiled and said, "No, I think we are fine."

Mia gave a soft smile and agreed, "Yes, everything is perfect."

Kate left and we ate our meals in silence, both of us coming to full terms with the revelations that had just been revealed. I knew now everything had changed. She loved me too. A serene feeling washed over me as I finally found peace with my inner turmoil over the seduction. She loved me. Mia loved me. I smiled to myself. I looked at Mia who had a radiant glow herself. I hoped she was having a similar joy inside herself.

We finished our meal, the wine bottle over half empty, and Kate came to take our plates. She asked, "How was your meal?"

"Delicious," I said.

Mia teased, "But probably not as delicious as you."

I smirked as that is something I would have usually used to push the envelope.

Kate, for the first time, responded to our sexual wordplay, "I have never had any complaints."

"I imagine that is true." Mia said, "I think it would be the perfect dessert."

Kate blushed, looked around and then said, "I would love to, but I can't, not here."

I could have taken control at this point, but I decided to watch and see how Mia played this.

Mia said, "Well the offer stands Kate. You are a very pretty woman, and you would make a great plaything for me and my girlfriend."

'Well played' I though thought to myself. It showed that she was in control and would be in this sexual relationship."

Kate smiled, leaned in and whispered, "How did you know I was gay?"

Mia smiled, "You kept checking out my breasts and my lover's legs."

"Oh," Kate said, "I have not come out yet to anyone."

"Well," Mia said teasingly, "Now you have."

Kate smiled and said, "I will be right back with your desserts."

She left and I said, "That was very well played Mia. I could not have done it any better myself."

"Well I learned from the master," she complimented. So," she paused and nervously asked, "now what?"

"We have dessert, we get a taxi, I am way too drunk to drive home, and then we go back to my place and I make love to you in a way you can not even begin to imagine."

Mia smiled seductively and said, "Trust me, I have imagined it in every way possible."

Kate returned with our chocolate cheese cake and gave Mia a piece of paper. Mia opened it up, smiled and said, "I will be in contact, sweetheart."

"I hope so," Kate responded.

Mia then said, "Want to see something really cool?"

"Sure," Kate said with a bit of trepidation.

Mia then pulled out something from her purse and said watch this. I recognized what it was just as she turned it on to full blast. Instantly, the vibrations sped up extremely and in only seconds my cunt exploded with an orgasm. I barely kept the sound to an escaped moan as the pleasure was amazing.

Mia then said to me, "Slut, could you please give your toy to Kate here."

I was shocked by Mia's name calling, but also incredibly turned on, as I ripped by slightly damp pantyhose open at the crotch and removed the very wet ball. I handed it obediently to Kate.

Kate quickly grabbed it and slid it in her pocket.

Mia said, "I expect that inside you in the next few minutes. I will turn it on low for you. I will retrieve it tomorrow."

"Yes ma'am," Kate obeyed and left the table.

Mia looked at me and said, "Sorry, I didn't mean to call you a slut."

I smiled, "You fucking bitch, I didn't know you had it in you."

Mia laughed, "I think you are in for many surprises."

"It seems I am," I said as I took a bite out of the cheesecake.

We ate in silence as both of us reflected on what was going to happen next. Kate came back with the bill and a devious smile. Mia asked, "I assume you have put my present in a safe place?"

"The safest there is," Kate flirted back.

Mia looked at the bill and then asked, "Was that number you gave me your cell number?"

"Yes ma'am," she answered.

"Do you work tomorrow?"

"No."

"Good, I will text you an address and I expect you to meet me there at 2PM," Mia instructed.

"Yes ma'am," Kate answered.

"And," Mia stressed, "We will be going to The Pheonix later in the evening, so be sure to wear something sexy and classy."

"Understood," Kate responded.

"And be sure to wear stockings, not pantyhose, I want easy access of my new slut."

Kate blushed at being called a slut, but said, "Yes ma'am." Mia then gave her a credit card. Kate left and we got ready to leave.

I said, "Mia you are a master manipulator."

She smiled, shot the last glass of wine, and said, "Let's get going, I've got one more present for you."

Kate returned, Mia signed the receipt, giving a very generous tip. She then stood up and whispered something into her ear.

Kate blushed again and said, "It was a pleasure serving you."

Mia responded wittily, "Wait till tomorrow, and then you can really say it was a pleasure serving me."

Kate smiled and said, "Have a good night."

Mia said and looked me directly in the eye, "Oh we will, won't we slut?"

Playing along, I answered, "Yes mistress."

Kate smiled, shook her head just slightly and left.

I grabbed Mia's hand and led her out of the restaurant. We hailed a taxi very quickly, gave him the address and instantly we were making out like two teenagers on a first date. The hormones raged as we kissed with such passion. The fire inside burned with such intensity, that I wanted to make love to her right in the taxi. My hand went under her dress and I rubbed her pussy gently and in only a few seconds Mia broke my kiss and had an intense orgasm. The taxi driver swerved the vehicle a bit, obviously surprised by the ecstatic sound of pleasure.

We went back to kissing until we arrived at my house. We got out of the cab, paid him and rushed into my house.

As soon as the door was closed, I pushed her against the wall and kissed her with reckless abandon. It was Mia who broke the kiss and said, "Wait, I need to give you your present."

"Can't it wait?" I said exasperated.

"No, I think it is crucial to give you now."

She then grabbed her bag and went to the bathroom. I nervously waited, eagerness overwhelming me. I had waited so long for this moment to happen and now that it was about too, my anxiety overwhelmed me. I paced the room as I waited for Mia to return.

Mia called, "Are you ready for your present?"

"Yes," I called frustrated, "Get out her now."

"Yes mistress," she responded to my surprise and opened the door. She walked out dressed in only tan thigh high stockings and two bows strategically placed on her two firm round voluptuous breasts. Her hair was in pigtails and she wore a collar around her neck with a leash she had in one hand. She walked over to me, handed me the leash and said, "I love you completely. I want to give you the best present I can think of, me. Not just for today, but for tomorrow and every other tomorrow. I am yours." She then dropped to her knees and waited my response.

In a million years, a trillion fantasies, I could not have imagined such a moment; such a sweet declaration; such a perfect submission. I looked down at my best friend, pulled her back up and kissed her. I then pushed her back down and led her by the leash to my bedroom. I laid her onto my bed and went to the closet and brought out my 'special' box. I took her left hand and handcuffed her to my bed; I then did the same to her right. She smiled as she watched me.

I then leaned down and kissed her neck. She gave a light moan the second my lips contacted her skin. I slowly, ever so slowly, moved my mouth down her body. I took off the bows that hid her stiff nipples and took each nipple into my mouth. I learned quickly her nipples were extremely sensitive as each nibble of her nipple had her breathing getting heavier. I slowly slid my tongue between her deliciously large breasts and then moved downwards, my tongue never leaving her body. My tongue reached her shaved treasure; I paused my lips a millimetre away from her ripe cunt, and then moved lower. She gave out a disappointed moan as my head left her eager pussy. My tongue then slid down her nylon clad left leg. I reached the sole of her foot and licked it. I then took each toe into my mouth and sucked it through the sheer nylon. Soft moans escaped my captive lover as I made love to her whole body. I then moved back up, again stopping at her already wet cunt and gave one quick lap of her clit. She gave a loud moan and begged, "Please more."

I looked up at her and said, "All in good time Mia."

I then moved down her right leg, repeating the same lengthy process. I spent an eternity sucking on her tiny, perfectly manicured toes. I then moved back to her pussy and gave her three quick licks. She moaned loudly again and I moved and kissed her again. She kissed me back and then I asked, "What do you want me to do next?"

She moaned, "Please dominate me. Treat me like you would one of your one night stand sluts."

"You sure?" I asked.

"Yes," she moaned, "I wasn't kidding when I said, I want to give myself to you completely."

"OK Mia," I said and reached into my collection and pulled out my we-vibe.

I turned on a vibrator and placed it at the entrance of her cunt, but not in. I then took off my dress and straddled my best friend's face. My pantyhose were still on, but I had ripped a hole big enough for her to access my pussy.

She began licking as best she could from her handcuffed position. Her moans from the pleasure of the teasing vibrator and the egg that was still inside her sent vibrations through her body. As she licked, I leaned forward and began sucking on her clit as she licked mine. In less than a minute of the triple pleasure, Mia screamed into my pussy, "I'm cumming." I kept pressure on her clit until her orgasm subsided and then moved back up.

Her licking had me close, but in this position I could not come, so I got off her face and, after taking the egg out of her cunt, put the feeldoe toy in her pussy. I then straddled the other end of the cock and began bouncing up and down on it. I moaned, "Fuck me Mia, fuck your best friend's cunt." Mia moved her ass up and down as best she could and I orgasmed after only a couple minutes of pleasure. I collapsed on top of her and we went back to kissing, the two ended vibrating toy still inside both of us. I undid the handcuffs, took off the leash and cuddled with her.

Mia said, "I love you so much."

I responded, "I love you more."

Mia said, "Will you fuck me?"

"I'd love too," I said, and went over to the box and put on one of my strap-on cocks, a smaller six inch one. I strapped it on and said, "Get on all fours."

"Yes mistress," she cooed.

"I like that slut. Beg for your mistress's cock?"

"Oh please, fuck me like the new lesbian I am. Pound my tight cunt that you now own."

I moved my cock to the entrance of her vaginal canal; I rubbed the cock around her entrance, teasing her.

She begged, "Please shove it in. Fuck me like your other whores."

With that I slid the cock in and began fucking her. I started slow, my hands on her waist. I asked, "How does my cock feel in you dyke?"

"So goooood," she responded.

"Is it better than Scott's cock?" I asked.

"So much better," she replied, "Please, fuck me harder; fill my cunt with your cock."

I began pumping the 6 inch toy in and out faster and deeper, eventually allowing the whole cock to disappear into my beautiful friend's pussy.

"Don't stop, please, never stop fucking me," she screamed as she climaxed from the fast paced fucking. I kept fucking her not slightly slowing down as the orgasm shook her body. I finally stopped fucking her and slipped out of the strap-on.

I then put on the slim, anal ready, strap-on cock. I lubed it up and asked, "Are you ready for complete submission to me?"

"I will never disobey you," she said, still on my bed on all fours.

"I recall you said you would never take anything in your ass."

"I did say that," she said.

"What do you say now?" I questioned.

"I say that I was wrong and you were right; never say never. Please take my anal cherry," Mia said.

I got behind her and slowly, gently, slid the toy into her ass. Mia leaned forward and put her head on a pillow to deal with the slight discomfort. I let the slim cock sit in her half way and then said, "OK butt slut, I want you to slowly move your perfect little ass back on my cock."

Mia moved back slowly, as I leaned back on my hind legs. I allowed Mia to move back on the cock at her own pace. Slowly Mia moved back, taking all five inches of the small vibe in her ass. She then began slowly moving back and forth on the cock. Her moaning began and she said, "Fuck, that feels good. I couldn't imagine this could feel like this." She began moving faster, her slightly chubby ass colliding with my body as she tried to get the cock deeper in her ass. Watching my once innocent friend turn into a complete ass slut was fucking hot. This scene kept on for a few minutes until my leg started going numb.

I pushed her forward and stood up. "Sorry Mia, my leg was losing its feeling."

She looked at me and said, "That was amazing."

I reached into the box and grabbed the double ended dildo I had bought with her. I said to her, "I have never tried this before."

Mia grabbed it, turned it on high, and slid it into her pussy, I then straddled the other end awkwardly and we pushed the cock inside me. We both moaned land moved forward until the long wide dildo disappeared inside our two pussies. Soon we were grinding our cunts together and feeling the vibrating dildo teasing our cunts. The sensations were thrilling as we both used each other to get off. The crazy intense pleasure continued for many minutes until we both orgasmed within seconds of each other. We collapsed on the bed, the dildo still deep inside both of us.

Finally I pulled the dildo out of both of us and lay down on the bed. I cuddled Mia and said, "I love you, happy Valentine's Day."

She whispered back exhausted, "I love you too Claire."

I kissed her neck, pulled the blankets over both of us and fell asleep with the woman I love the most in my arms.

Did you love *Lesbian Love Songs*? Then you should read *Getaway Island*[1] by Lee Cushing!

[2]

They were promised a peaceful vacation. Now they're fighting for their lives.

Determined to put her past behind her, werewolf and former supernatural operative Catherine McBride is eager to enjoy a much-needed vacation with the woman she loves. But when a pair of resort guests is found brutally murdered, they're quickly catapulted into a sinister mystery with terrifying consequences.Daphne is dead-set on unravelling the truth behind the murders... despite her wife Catherine's protests. Teaming up with her charming – and magnetically attractive – fellow field operative Rachel, Daphne plunges headlong into a puzzling investigation that unearths rumors of missing

---

1. https://books2read.com/u/38VLR6

2. https://books2read.com/u/38VLR6

hearts and secretive cults. But as tensions rise, accusations run wild and her relationship with Catherine is stretched to the breaking point. Daphne is forced into an impossible situation: continue searching for the truth, or repair her bond with Catherine while she still can. But before she's able to make a choice, Daphne stumbles into a horrifying reality that changes everything...

Read more at https://www.goodreads.com/author/show/4203478.Lee_Cushing..

Also by Lee Cushing

Trust Casefiles
The Trust Casefiles
Pack Hunters
The Girls Of Lakeview Academy
Tourist Trap
The Brides Of Bathory
The President's Daughter
Vladek
Flesh & Blood
Getaway Island

Standalone
The Other Woman
Heart Of Love, Heart Of Darkness
Demon Vengeance
The Voodoo Mambo
Blood Prey
Her First Time
The No Kill List
Horror Geek Vampire Slayers
When Vampire Romances Go Bad
The Gorgon Abduction

The Bully
The Karnstein Pendant
The Vampire & The Virgin
Freshmen
The Dragons Of The Misty Highlands
The Princess
Rex Ryder - Bounty Hunter
A Thousand Reasons
The Wraith
Lesbian Love Songs
Night Tales

Watch for more at https://www.goodreads.com/author/show/
4203478.Lee_Cushing..